CW00457685

She Left Her Heart in China

The Story of Dr Sally Wolfe
Medical Missionary 1915 – 1951

by

JANE WRIGHT

Cloverhill Press

She Left Her Heart in China

Published by:
Cloverhill Press
57, Main Street
Groomsport
Co Down
1999

ISBN 0 9536122 0 1

© copyright Jane Wright. All rights reserved. No part of this publication may be reproduced, stored in a retrieval system or transmitted, in any way, without the prior permission of the copyright owner.

Typeset by December Publications

Front Cover:
Dr Sally Wolfe MB, BCh, BAO (NUI)
Photo by Hilda Porter

Back Cover:
Sally's address in Hankow, Hupeh Province

ACKNOWLEDGEMENTS

I would like to thank the following for their help in the research and production of this book:

Dr Sally Wolfe's nieces and nephews in Canada, especially Mrs Marjorie Christmas, Mrs Linda Rodger and Mrs Mona Kriss who were so generous in providing me with letters and photographs.

The Reverend Tom and Mrs Gillian Kingston, the late Reverend George Good, the Reverend Desmond and Mrs Kit Gilliland and Mrs Marion Kelly. Also, Bill Wright, Miss Susan Cooke, Dr Lorna Johnston, Mrs Elizabeth Appleby, Mrs Avesia Brien, Mr John Boles, Miss Nancy Yates, Mrs Rosemary Evans, Mrs Doreen McBride, the archivists of University College, Cork, and Glasgow University and Mr Howard Watson, Permissions Controller of Random House UK Ltd, who gave permission for the extracts from *China, my China.*

Finally, I would like to thank most particularly Professor Finlay Holmes who kindly read the script for me and gave me such valuable advice therein.

CONTENTS

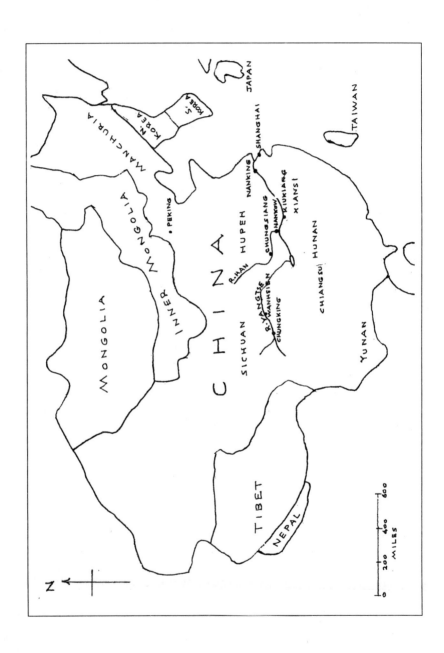

CHAPTER ONE

Early Life

Dr Sally Wolfe died on 15th July, 1975, aged ninety. After her funeral, my mother, who was her eldest niece, went to collect her possessions from St Luke's, the nursing home in Cork city where she had spent the last few years of her life. She was handed a worn, well-travelled brown trunk.

I don't recall absolutely everything that was in that trunk but I do remember that we were all deeply moved by the sheer simplicity of its contents. It was at once apparent that Sally had pared her life down to the minimum, not because she couldn't afford possessions or because people didn't look after her properly, but because she chose to live simply. She had a Bible and a hymn book and a portable typewriter and a selection of clothes. There were two or three of the white, woollen crocheted caps which she always wore but there were no frivolities and particularly striking was the absolute absence of such things as photographs, souvenirs and letters. She did own a Chinese Bible and a Chinese Methodist hymn book and I suppose they were in the trunk but if so they would have constituted the only things that were at all unusual. Looking at the general contents of that trunk, one would have been forgiven if one had thought that the owner had been little more than a pious old lady.

Which, of course, was far from the case. Born into a fairly well-to-do Methodist family from West Cork, clever and extremely beautiful, Sally had at an early stage in her life decided that she wanted to be a medical missionary and that God was calling her to go to China.

Eventually, over thirty years of her life were spent in that country, years of constant political upheaval through all of which she worked unremittingly to

The Grove, Skibbereen.

bring better health to the Chinese people. She adopted three orphaned Chinese children but had to leave them behind when she left the country in 1951. That was twenty-four years before she died and during those twenty-four years, as far as I know, she never received one word from or about those children. It must have been a great grief to her, yet she never spoke of it and very seldom mentioned her time in China at all, preferring to live stoically and calmly in the present and not to burden others with her sorrows. Indeed, if one asked her anything about that time, she would reply "Oh, that was a very long time ago" and immediately change the subject.

To learn anything about her life one had to wait therefore for those unguarded moments when she might mention some aspect of her missionary experience but those times were rare and none of us wrote down what she said. Luckily, however, some of her letters have survived, having been kept by the recipients, and I have been able to use these to piece together her story. There are not very many of them, given the length of time she spent in China, which suggests she was an infrequent correspondent. Moreover, these letters, in keeping with her personality, tend to understate the role she played.

Sarah Christine (she always preferred to be called Sally) was born on Christmas Day, 1885, the second child and eldest daughter of John Joseph Wolfe of Skibbereen and his wife Marion, *née* Bennett. I am not sure exactly where she was born but at some stage in Sally's early childhood they moved into The Grove, a house which lies just outside Skibbereen and which had been her grandmother Wolfe's childhood home.

Both the Wolfes of Skibbereen and the Bennetts of Clonakilty were successful flour millers and John Joseph also farmed. The Grove is a fairly substantial, late Georgian house and life was comfortable. Sally received her early education in Skibbereen, first at the Ladies' School and then at Mr Storey's Intermediate School, where she and her sister Fan always sat at the front. Finally, she went to Alexandra College in Dublin before entering Cork University to study medicine in 1908.

There were strong religious overtones in her early life and her parents both came from committed Methodist families. Each of Sally's grandfathers had pledged enormous sums of money to the Methodist church. Her paternal grandfather, William Wolfe of Ilen House, Skibbereen, undertook to give the church £400 a year, a promise he kept even when financial ruin hit him after

Sally – just before she went to university.

two cargoes of wheat, which he had bought in advance, were lost at sea in quick succession. He had been planning to build a conservatory on to his house but this was never done, owing to the financial collapse. His payments to the church, however, never faltered.

Thomas Bennett of Shannonvale, Clonakilty, her maternal grandfather, made a similar pledge, paying £400 for four years to augment the stipends of Methodist ministers and £200 a year for a period of six years to help the Home Mission Fund. Mr Bennett created a chapel at Shannonvale, where he himself held lay services every Sunday afternoon. This was not a particularly unusual practice - prominent Methodist men in both towns travelled miles on Sunday afternoons to hold services in outlying places, sometimes in small Methodist churches and sometimes in people's homes.

Thus the atmosphere in which Sally grew up was rich in faith and good works. Her decision to be a missionary, therefore, is quite understandable but that decision cannot have been an easy one. For a start, her father seems to have been against the idea of her going to China. We know that he made her promise not to do so until she was thirty, a promise she kept.

Then there was her medical training, a career choice that was fairly avant garde for a woman at the time. She graduated from University College, Cork, in 1913. (She was not one of the first female medical graduates of that College, as has sometimes been claimed. University College, Cork was graduating women doctors as early as the 1890's).

Her record there is impressive - she was First Year Exhibitioner in Science 1907-08, Second Year Exhibitioner 1909, got a Fourth Year Scholarship of £28 in 1910-11 and a Fifth Year Scholarship of £30 in 1912. Her father had died in 1905, and there were financial difficulties, so the scholarships must have been useful. There were five children altogether in the family and her elder brother, William, had to cut short his training as an electrical engineer in order that Sally could complete hers. He did so willingly, in view of the fact that she wished to be a missionary.

The first surviving letter we have from her concerns a graduation ceremony, the First Degree Congregation. Writing on 28th May, 1910 to her brother, William Wolfe, she is characteristically brief about the ceremony:

> The first degrees were conferred here on Wednesday. There were
> six of them. But the professors etc came in in a very imposing

procession, in all the colours of the rainbow, and the President made a speech. Then Dr Moore, dean of Medicine, made a short Latin speech and presented the candidates, whom he designated 'meos filios', for their degrees, which the President conferred, also in Latin. Then they all went out and so did we.

Her words 'the first degrees' refer to a truly historic occasion. Up until 1908, the Universities of Dublin, Cork and Galway had been known as the Queen's Colleges and their examinations and degrees had been under the jurisdiction of what was known as 'The Royal University.' In 1908, the Irish Universities' Act established the National University of Ireland with three constituent colleges - Dublin, Cork and Galway.

The President of University College, Cork, Dr Windle, conferred the first degrees of the new University on 25th May, 1910. Sally, it seems, was present as a spectator at this ceremony, though she was not a recipient since she did not qualify until 1913. (The University records list her as a Third Year student in 1909-10). From her wry comment it would seem that at least one of the six graduates she mentions must have been a woman. Perhaps they all were.

It seems to have been a time of trouble in Cork itself. Her letter mentions ranks of policemen lining Patrick Street when she came out of the Wesley Chapel on the following Sunday morning and they were doing the same that evening. She writes of police standing shoulder to shoulder and also on horseback and there were groups of them with guns placed in Academy Street. Two baton charges occurred and the infirmaries were full of the resultant scalp wounds, though not all that were seen were caused by the police. She saw some of these in the South Infirmary, to which she was presumably attached as a medical student. She also saw a man who had been stabbed in the forearm. Stab wounds, she says, are a rarity and the offenders, if caught, always end up in court.

Her first known medical appointment was in Glasgow, at the Royal Samaritan Hospital where she was a resident house surgeon in 1913. The appointment was an unpaid one, though she got her keep. The Honorary Secretary of the hospital wrote to her in May 1913 to tell her that there would be a vacancy in August and that the appointment would last for six months. The letter was sent to her at Citadella, Blackrock Rd, Cork. This was

Graduation: Sally is in the centre of the back row.

the home of her cousin, Miss Nannie Wolfe, and I suspect she had stayed with that cousin throughout her time at Cork University.

In June 1913, the Honorary Secretary again wrote to her. Her address this time was The Hospice, High Street, Edinburgh, which I imagine was probably a hotel or guest house. This is what he said:

> The vacancy…is in Dr Russell's own Wards, and in view of his strong recommendation, I think that I can venture to say that if you desire the appointment and send me your application at once you would be almost certain to obtain it…I may say that the Medical Committee are delaying the public announcement of the vacancy in order to give you an opportunity of applying….

Dr A. W. Russell, Surgeon to the Royal Samaritan Hospital for Women, was also Examiner in Midwifery and Gynaecology for the National University of Ireland, so it would seem reasonable to suppose that it was through him that she applied for this post. If so, his belief in her was not matched by her belief in him, as you will see.

On 16th June the Honorary Secretary wrote to her in Edinburgh to inform her that her application had been successful and to tell her that:

> Your duties will be principally to attend the patients in the Wards under Drs A. W. Russell and David Shannon's charge and…to see the patients that may be waiting at the Dispensary [i.e. the Out-patients Department]

Sally wrote about her experiences in the hospital in a letter dated 12th November, 1913, which she sent to her mother, who was living in Alberta in Canada. Most of her family had gone there by then, having left The Grove and had gone 'homesteading'; that is, choosing and developing their own virgin farmland. This letter announced that she had given in her resignation.

One gets the distinct impression that the arrival of this intelligent, keen young woman doctor was not relished by the older medics in the hospital - she says 'there is no sympathy between us' and that she is 'glad to be getting out.' She got on well, though, with the two other young house surgeons but found sharing a sitting room with them sometimes embarrassing:

> When visitors come (young fellows they knew at college) my position is a little awkward. They all wish I was not there and so do I. But how to leave a room gracefully is a very difficult problem.

Much worse, though, is the frustration of the job:

> I had another row with Dr Russell last week and I was very rude to him in public. It was a pity but I just lost my temper altogether. I had a patient who died and it so happened that I had hit on the treatment she ought to have. She needed immediate operation. So I rang up Dr Russell and asked whether he would come over and see her, as if not I wished to get Dr Campbell. I would much have preferred Dr Campbell, however we have to take them in the appointed order!
>
> Dr Russell came over and I took him to see her. Really, it was just my luck or some good angel that put it into my head, for I did not know at all what was up but I just dropped on the right thing and on three good reasons for doing it.
>
> Dr Russell, on the other hand, did not know what to do, so he did nothing. "If it is as you say," he said, "things will soon develop and we'll see." So I said "Yes, it will soon shew and then it will be too late to do anything." So I besought him to operate and he just would not. Said I, with my experience, could not possibly diagnose what he with his experience failed to and so forth. Told me, in effect, that I was cheeky and conceited. That was Saturday afternoon. He said he would come round on Sunday.
>
> I was so angry, I nearly cried that day in the sitting room and Drs McVey and Paterson comforted me, and said I had done all I could do and my hands were clean, anyway. I said if I had her in the heart of the Sahara, I could treat her myself but just because she was in Glasgow in a surgical hospital, she had to die untreated.
>
> Five hours later I rang Dr Russell up to report progress and everything

that could have happened had happened and death was imminent and I told him what I had told him before and he said "Well, there isn't any use in my coming over" and I said "No, I don't think there is any." That was 11 o'clock at night and she died at 4 a.m.

On Monday morning, Dr Russell was telling Dr Campbell about it. "It is the suddenness that is so terrible," he said, so I spun round on him. "Dr Russell, I told you on Friday I did not consider that woman well and you did not look at her" I said, very bitterly. And he said, on the defence immediately, "Ah, but Sister told me afterwards that she was all right." It is true - Sister Brown had taken it on herself to tell him that, immediately I had said the other. It was cheek of her but it did not exculpate him.

I did not reply to that defence and I never nowadays bring Sister Brown into my rows with the chiefs. She is the cause of most of them but not of all. But I am in the superior position and it is my reports they ought to take and not hers and she has no right whatever to contradict my reports.

Then Russell went on to say that "It would not have mattered anyway, that the woman would have died whatever he had done" and Dr Campbell said "Some of these cases do awfully well if you drain them." That finished me. I knew it, too. There had been one chance of that woman's life and he had refused.

So I said, with venom to Dr Campbell "She was not drained until half an hour before she died, she burst her wound" and I nearly cried again, I was so angry about it. And Dr Russell said "Did I think it would have made any difference?" Then I was a little sorry for him, so I said "No, I didn't suppose it would," which was only half true.

It would have made all the difference in the world to my thought of him, though. For it is terrible to think that little as I know at this time of my life, he, who is about 50 or so and has been or thinks he has been a surgeon for ages, knows less and has to be told what to do and won't even see it when he is told to do it.

I rang him on Sunday and invited him over to inspect the body p.m. - said I did not want a post mortem but would like him to come over and see me open up her wound. It was tremendous

The Wolfe family: Sally's mother in the centre, with Tom and Fan seated and standing (from left) Sally, Willie and Kitty.

cheek. But he would not come and forbade me to touch her wound, unless the husband wished for a post mortem. I did not ask the husband. So we had none and we did not need it.

Poor old Dr Russell. And I have been quite good to him and he is afraid of his life of Dr McVey, who will be his house surgeon next month. Dr McVey says the Fiscal ought to interfere and cancel Dr Russell's licence to practise, as he had been directly responsible for so many deaths. Dr McVey had him in Maternity and is absolutely merciless. He says he saw Dr Russell directly do such and such things and does not forget…he (Dr Russell) is a mean man and a fool and he deserves to be treated as such and he (Dr McVey) means to treat him.

I am rather sorry for Dr Russell, for both Paterson and McVey know him. I invited him into the sitting room today. He was going to dictate some reports for me and I thought we could do them quite nicely there. He said "No, I won't go there, those boys will be there." Poor old man. He is quite sorry to lose me, as he anticipates worse trouble ahead."

But I am quite glad to be clear of them all,

Sally

Even before she wrote this letter, Sally must have been expressing dissatisfaction with things, for the Honorary Secretary wrote to her on September 19th saying:

> I do not know how the rumour you refer to has reached you. The question of reducing the resident staff from the present three to two is not at present before the Directors…. As far as you personally are concerned your appointment does not expire until the end of January and … the Directors would much regret, should you really desire from any cause to leave before the termination of your engagement.

Despite this letter, Sally resigned on 30th November and the Honorary Secretary wrote to her in December at The Corner House, Skibbereen (the home of her sister, Fan), saying that the Directors wished to express their high appreciation of her services and to wish her all the best in her future.

CHAPTER TWO

China

Happier times lay ahead for Sally, as two letters dated October 1915 show. By then she had been in China for six months (having spent part of the interim time visiting her relations in Canada), was working in the Jubilee Women's Hospital at the Wesleyan Mission in Hankow, had passed her first exam in Chinese with ease (getting 93 per cent), and was full of excited interest in all that was going on around her.

There were other young European women at the Mission - Miss Nora Booth, who was the matron of the hospital and had charge of the nurses (mainly Chinese) and Miss Ethel Wagstaff, a newcomer like herself. At some stage she had her photograph taken with these two and with two others called Alice Shackleton and Florence Gooch. They appear to be all about her age.

On arrival in China, with fellow missionaries: from left Ethel Wagstaff, Nora Booth, Alice Shackleton, Florence Gooch and Sally Wolfe.

Her letters concern the betrothal ceremony of one of the Chinese nurses in the hospital and the marriage of another one and were written to her sister Kitty and her mother, both in Canada.

The first part of the letter about the betrothal is unfortunately missing - she appears to have been telling her young sister about Chinese etiquette when entertaining important guests:

...at the same feast, for each must be top. However, we had no such complications, for Mrs Wang was the only important person present. And further, the feast was not purely Chinese, it was semi-foreign. I mean, they did not go in for elaborate Chinese manners. For one thing, everybody's name was written on a slip of red paper and put at her place and we just went and sat there.

Chinese etiquette is to place the most honoured guest first and in the best place. The guest, however, declines to sit there and seats himself somewhere else. I believe anywhere else will do, he protests he is unworthy to sit top and so forth. The host flatters him and insists, so after some palaver, the guest gets up and goes a little higher, probably sitting down again in another wrong seat. This sort of thing goes on a longer or shorter time according to the amount of politeness the guest feels called upon to show.

It is a complicated business to know which seat is best and the order in which the others come. The one thing that is certain is that the people who sit on each side of you do not rank next to you in importance. However, that does not matter, for the host knows the relative values of the seats and also the relative importance of the guests. If then he places the most important guest first and works down in order, you may assume that when it comes to your turn, you will be piloted to the best seat vacant and so it is politely humble to take any of the other empty places.

This is the idea so far as I have yet got hold of it. However, as I say, we did not do that yesterday, neither did we say "Puk ch'ih". It is polite to always refuse every eatable offered to you. You should say "Puk ch'ih", which means "I won't eat it." You may then take the bit in your chop sticks and give it to your neighbour, who may eat it or give it to somebody else or back to you. You ought not to help yourself to anything, but wait for somebody else to hand it to you. This, of course, he will do with his chop sticks or spoon. Yesterday, however, we were instructed not to be polite, because foreigners did not know how.

There were four tables, each sitting eight people. The table cloths (as a rule, there are none) were red. At each place was a tiny basin with a short-handled spoon lying in it. The spoon was china and like a dessert spoon. The basin was also china and just big enough to hold the bowl of the spoon.

On the table there were about a dozen small white plates of cold viands. I don't remember them all, nor did I know them all. One was olives, another divisions of small orange, another little bits of ham, about enough for two bites but cut very thin, and on this plate were also old eggs cut into eighths. Old eggs are eggs that have been buried in lime and earth for not less than 100 days. I do not know whether they are cooked or not. But they are almost black and there is hardly any difference between the look of the yolk and the white. The consistence is that of a hard-boiled egg and the flavour is like that of a hard-boiled egg and yet it is not quite the same.

That would make three plates. There were also dried fish in little bits and shrimps in their shells (I did not notice how anybody manipulated them), chicken boiled and in bites was another, sugar candy, dried Chinese dates (you never eat [sic] any like them) and a plate of monkey nuts, shelled and peeled and glazed with something, I suppose Chinese gelatine but do not know. Also a plate of round nuts…prepared in the same way….

Miss Booth says we ought to have loitered over these a bit. But I suppose, owing to the delay in the beginning, the hot dishes were ready and had to be served immediately. One came in directly the blessing was asked, that is four alike did, one for each table. Each dish is like a slop bowl. I don't know how many dishes there were. There was roast duck, tripe, crab, sea-slugs, shrimps out of their shells, pork, mushrooms and other things. They serve one bowl at a time.

That reminds me, we had two kinds of little steamed

dumplings… I rashly took one in my chop sticks, holding it about the middle. I bit off one end, and, of course, the whole collapsed and plumped into my basin. There is no very obvious reason why it should have hit on the basin but luckily it did.

Last of all rice came in. You must eat up the very last rice grain. For a long [time] I practised it. It is quite easy to eat the greater part of it, but the last grains are elusive and for several months I did not learn the knack…

… After it was over, someone asked Miss Booth what it cost. She said she had nothing to do with it and had not been told but it was not an expensive feast. She guessed it cost 4,500 or 5,000 cash a table. That is about 6/- for eight people. I was amazed, as I had thought it would be very much more. Though beef is about 2d a pound usually and quite good at that. So you see I am not likely to die from having to live on rice only. Pork is rather dearer.

Two weeks later, on 31st October, Sally wrote to her mother, describing the wedding of one of the other Chinese nurses:

Dear Mammy,

I expect you will think we are going in for great dissipation when I tell you we were at another feast yesterday.

The occasion was the marriage of one of our nurses, not the same one who was betrothed a fortnight ago. It was a great affair.

Miss Booth gave her nice little cups and saucers such as any house at home might have. They were really lovely, though quite cheap. The china was very nice. Also, she gave her a teapot which almost matched them. These were, of course, foreign style. I gave her Chinese saucers, ten of them. The Chinese set is 10, not 12.

It may seem funny to you to give saucers without cups, but it is all right here. The cup is a little basin, without any handle: it has a cover, just like a saucer, only its rim is smaller than that of the cup, so that it fits down a little way into it. It is put on, what would be upside down for one of our saucers. The cup, in better class houses, is brought to you standing in a little 'shee' saucer. I don't know how to spell 'shee' but that is the sound it has. It is a metal like very white brass and is used for lots of things. So I gave Lantaku 10 little metal saucers, with flowers cut on them. They cost 3, 800 cash, that is not quite 5/- in English money. Miss Gooch and Miss Booth thought it about right for me to give her. Some of the other nurses also approved of the suggestion.

The wedding was great. The husband is the eldest son of a family which is head of the clan, or whatever it would be. They are not wealthy but for such an individual, they had to have a big wedding, all the families contributed to it. They say there were 300 guests, or some people do: others say 30 tables and each table seats 8. Of course, we came in relays. There were only 4 tables in our room. It was not a very elaborate feast, there were just 12 cold things on the table and 7 hot served afterwards.

To finish up, we got tea, a lot of cups brought in on a tray and on the same tray a little bowl with a bit of red paper in it and some coins on it. I had been instructed beforehand, so knew what to do. You take a cup of tea and deposit on the tray or in the basin a little bundle of money done up in red paper. This is a tip for the cooks. Miss Booth asked some of our girls before we went and they advised 500 cash for us. I noticed that as far as I could see no-one else gave so much. However, of course, I was not going to open up my little bundle there and take out a few coins, so I gave it all. And, as Miss Booth says, they are rather poor and you have the consolation of knowing you more than paid for what you ate.

Each guest must give at least 500 cash or a present of that value. So it is not altogether an expense to give a big wedding. And they count on the cooks tips, too. Miss Booth says, cooks will come in and provide everything very cheaply if you agree to let them have this money. If you like, however, you can bargain with your caterers for the feast and keep all the money so given yourself. So you do not know whether it is the host or the caterer who runs the sporting chance.

This nurse of ours was what they call "a little daughter-in-law." That is to say, she had gone to live with her husband's family as a child, so of course, the marriage was altogether in their hands.

I wish it were not such a fag to write. The bride wore pink silk, Chinese dress and shoes, with Miss Booth's veil and orange blossoms and carried a bunch of pink roses, kindly contributed by the Hanyang boarding school. This bouquet was adorned with a blue silk sash, which the bridegroom presented for the purpose. Two of the other nurses were bridesmaids. For some reason or other, there was only one best man, the custom is two but one failed to turn up at the critical moment. The Chinese as a rule have married men to act this part and also however many "bridesmaids" there are, in foreign fashion, there is always a married woman to accompany the bride and stay with her through the day.

The church was decorated in a style which doubtless pleased the parties concerned. It was done entirely by the bridegroom's friends. I did not admire it. It was a little like a poor shop at home at Christmas - lots of gaudy paper and some green: bamboo and cypress as far as I could make out.

The blind organist played. But in addition, there was a band. A huge drum, several flutes, a triangle, a cymbal and perhaps some other things. The band stood beside the organ and did nothing during the service. At the end, the bride and bridegroom meekly stood in front of the communion rail and waited. It seemed an age to me. But the band wished to play a march for them to go out to and there was some hitch about getting started.

If I was one of the contracting parties, I think I would have given up and walked out without it. However, they got the band, I think, all the way from Wuchang for the purpose, so they waited. And, after a time, they struck up in great style. Our folks expected it would be 'Yankee Doodle', which they say is a great favourite but it was not, it was 'Rosalie, the Prairie Flower.' And the happy couple immediately began to walk out, to strains of what is really a very good wedding march.

It distressed Ethel. She thought Mr Sutton ought not to have allowed the band in the church. It did not worry me, and all the Chinese seemed to think a lot of it. Apparently, you are no end a great man if you have a band to play for you.

The Chinese have no ceremonial marriage. They just announce the marriage and give a feast. So all the ceremony is foreign.

Mr Sutton asked for the ring, which the bridegroom produced. A Chinese bridegroom gives the bride two bracelets and two rings. They are given at betrothal and bargained for before that is completed. They are ornamental rings, rather nice usually. Ethel, who is in this respect a duffer, thinks we should get them to use plain rings, like we do for weddings.

Anyway, I was saying Mr Sutton told the bridegroom to say "With this ring, I thee wed" or something on that line. I did not hear what he said and would not have understood, anyway. The bridegroom said something and dumped the ring into the bride's hand. Mr Sutton then explained that he was to slip it on the bride's finger, pointing out which finger. So he then made one dive at it and got it about halfway on, where he left it. It was rather funny. He did not make them take hands at all, I don't know whether he could have. They seemed to be determined to stand far away from each other and when they left the church, he just walked out and the bride followed a little way behind.

Men and women sit apart in church and most people think the reason we don't get better class women to church is that we have no partition. They say women won't sit where men can stare at them.

Altogether, the sexes are much more separated than at home. They rarely sit at one table, never at a feast. Yesterday there was a room for men and a room for women. But afterwards they put one table of men in our room. I think it was because there were so many foreigners there and Mr Clayton had come in, when there was no room for him in the men's room. So, not to keep him waiting too long, they got together the bridegroom and several teachers and made up 8 for a table in our room. I fancy we were either second or third to be fed. But it was a sort of running feast, when a table emptied, they seated 8 more.

It was a very funny sort of room. The household is heathen, notwithstanding the wedding in church. (Both bride and groom have had Christian teaching but neither is baptised). There was a shrine in one corner. There were also ancestral tablets. The floor was earth, the walls rough wood on three sides, or so I thought. The fourth side had no wall, or if you like to say so it had a stone wall but the roof stopped short about 3 or 4 yards from it. There were no windows. The light came through the open side. I cannot give you any idea what it was like. It did not belong to the family but was hired from a neighbour for the day.

The bride sat upstairs all day, everyone spoke to her. There was nothing objectionable while we were in her presence but they say later on, when people get a little drunk, she has to put up with a lot. That girls usually cry all the day before and the day after. That is the one day when a woman must see outside men, who are often insolent to her. However, her woman attendant is supposed to stay with her all along.

The stairs was a ladder and very dark. I found it quite hard to step on to it to come down. There was no rail up from the bottom. Miss Booth was worried because a kindly lady would hold up her dress as she came down, for fear it should get soiled. Chinese do spit about worse than Americans…. No one held up my dress for me and I got down all right.

The bride probably wore pink as a compromise between red and white. Red was the colour of felicity usually worn by Chinese brides but white, which Westerners wore, was the Chinese colour of mourning and would never be worn. The way she was exposed to all those drunken comments seems very cruel to us but it was part of the Chinese marriage custom for men to 'tease' the bride, to test her character: if she cried or spoke out she would be considered bad-tempered.

Sally enclosed her invitation to the wedding in this letter. The red invitation was addressed to 'Wu Shen Sa.' Wu was her Chinese surname and 'Shen' (teacher) and 'Sa' (firstborn) were the two Chinese first names which were appropriate to her. Sally said in this letter that she felt 'Doctor, born to heal' would have been a better name.

She didn't give her mother an explanation as to how her Chinese name had been chosen. There is always a problem in translating European names into Chinese as no straight translation is possible, there being no Chinese alphabet as such. Anyway, European names are very difficult for Chinese people to pronounce and, even if there had been an easy way to get a translation, it would most likely have been avoided.

Instead of an alphabet, there are thousands of 'characters' which denote meaning but not phonetics. Obviously, there are a great many of them: the translation of the Bible, for instance, contains 5,000. There are specific characters for the 'one hundred names' that are used as surnames in China and out of these the mission chose 'Wu' to be Sally's, for obvious reasons. Names are very meaningful to the Chinese and each of her three would have been chosen with care.

The surviving letters give no description of the city of Hankow. However, her contemporary, Harold B. Rattenbury, who was based in the Wesleyan Mission as a teaching member, wrote graphically about Hankow in his book *China, my China.* He describes it as being one of three great cities that grew up where the River Han joins the Yangtse River and explains that its name means 'Han Mouth.' The other two cities are Hanyang and Wuchang and the three together are generally referred to as 'the Wu-Han' cities. Hankow and Wuchang are separated by more than a mile of water, even though at this point the Yangtse river is 600 miles from the port of Shanghai and the sea. Hankow, he says, was the biggest of the three cities, with a population of more than a million.

It was also the most 'modern' of the cities. It had a Custom House, many important banks such as the Hong Kong Bank, several shipping buildings and numerous consulates, each one of which flew a national flag. Seven miles of the swampiest river area was reserved for foreign consulates and their business enterprises, the area being known as 'The Concessions.' Many international firms operated from Hankow, with names such as Butterfield & Matheson, Jardines, and Swires, as well as a totally Chinese firm called 'The China Merchants'. These firms sent steamers up and down the Yangtse, carrying freight in their holds and passengers on their decks. The missionaries did not live in The Concessions but in the heart of Chinese Hankow itself. However, they always travelled first class on these steamers, that being an unwritten rule. The decks below were reserved for four classes of Chinese.

The river was packed with thousands of other boats. There were rice boats, each with a basket hanging from its mast to indicate the cargo, fuel boats with logs at their mastheads and coal boats which served a double purpose: they brought coal and coal dust down from the province of Hunan and when they had delivered their cargo, their timbers would be broken up for the building trade. Amongst all these would be other boats - boats with people living on them and tiny sampans ferrying people about and junks selling goods such as crockery and groceries to those boat people. From his residence, which was in the Mission and situated next to Sally's hospital, Harold Rattenbury could see 'scores and hundreds' of these boat masts. Whether Sally could see them from the hospital is, of course, not known, but it would be a view she would be quite familiar with as she came and went through the town.

Harold Rattenbury gives very evocative descriptions of the street life in Hankow. Sally's hospital and the General Hospital across the street opened directly on to the main thoroughfare. This street was called the 'Cheng Chien' or 'True Street.'
This is how he described it:

> There were coolies swinging heavy-laden baskets on their shoulder-poles, bearing rice, vegetables, pots and pans, bricks, lime, and every conceivable thing of weight. There were other coolies with great tree-trunks on their shoulders and occasionally a freshly painted coffin came swinging along on the backs of men. The coolies sang their "Hey-hoh-ti, hey-how-ti" which…helped them at their work. There was continuous movement up and down the street which was never by day or night completely still.

Other bare-backed coolies carried water in wooden buckets, one on either end of their poles, which they delivered to houses in the Chinese part of the town, there being no water supply laid on. Rickshaws jostled with these and with other passers-by, most of whom were men, though there were also some 'blue-gowned grannies with hobbled feet.' There was a drain down the middle of the Cheng Chien, as there was in every street, into which all the slops and garbage from the adjoining buildings was thrown, (though not, I am sure, from the two hospitals). Lesser streets opened off the Cheng Chien and led to a mass of alleys where it was very easy to get lost. One street was a chopstick street, selling nothing but chopsticks.

The Cheng Chien was about four miles long and narrow, with shops

A Chinese granny, whose feet have been bound in childhood, being led by a child.

along both sides. Most shops sold specialist goods - silks, medicines, shark fins, glazed ducks, sweet hams, groceries, stationery and every type of Chinese porcelain. There were fruit shops selling bananas, melons, oranges and dried fruits. Money changers sat plying their trade behind their little brass grills. There were plenty of tea shops and barbers shops and shops that sold Chinese crackers, which the Chinese let off on festive occasions.

There were many 'cash paper' shops, where the Chinese could go to buy symbolic money, which they burnt in their temples, believing it was thus transmuted to the dead in the spirit world. Cash paper was yellow and was made out of bamboo. Apprentices sat all day long in these shops, punching holes in the squares of cash paper - the holes represented those found in the strings of coin that had been used in former times. Other shops sold tissue paper and bamboo furniture, horses, boxes, houses and figures of people - all things that would be similarly useful to the dead when burnt and thus sent on to them.

The shops opened directly on to the street and had no windows but at night they would be closed in with shutters. Often, half their goods spilled out on to the street. Other people set up little stalls out on the roadside, selling such things as live fish which were kept in wooden tubs, or offering passers-by the chance to have their fortune told and all the time a ceaseless crowd of people moved up and down the street so that all was, in Harold Rattenbury's words:

> ...noise, noise, noise as sweating, sturdy coolies with their rice
> and vegetables balanced on their carrying poles, trotted along,
> jostling with the rickshaws and the passers-by, shouting to clear
> the way and make room for the burden-bearer.

The missionaries adjusted to this thronging street life. It was impossible to preach in the crowded street itself, so they set up their own preaching rooms, opening off the Cheng Chien, into which they attracted the tired and the curious, offering them bench seats and quiet. Here they patiently preached and talked all day long. Sometimes people went away, unmoved, but sometimes they listened and were converted. A Chinese gate-keeper sat at the door opening on to the street and had a little stall, with books for sale which the interested ones could buy.

Harold Rattenbury says these street chapels were more influential than might be thought and that many had their first taste of what Christianity was about in these chapels. It is almost certain that Sally never preached in any of these, being a medical missionary. She was a bit diffident about her teaching skills but did, of course, run Bible classes in her hospital for the women and children and would have taken a deep interest, no doubt, in the work going on outside. She had arrived in the country at an exciting time for a would-be missionary, for Harold Rattenbury says the years 1911-27 were extremely fertile ones from the point of view of the conversion of the Chinese people to Christianity.

The next surviving letter from Sally is dated 21st September, 1918 and is to her mother, Marion Wolfe, in Canada. The First World War was still in progress in Europe and Sally's youngest brother Tom, who had been living in Canada, had volunteered for the front. Sally informs her mother that she is handstitching him a couple of silk handkerchiefs for his birthday. Someone has told her that these would have to be khaki and so she is doing her best. One handkerchief is a dark colour, with flowers on it, and it is quite large but the second handkerchief will be smaller (14 inches square), due to the narrowness of the silk.

Most of the letter, however, is taken up with a distressing incident:

> I think I told you about Kao Nai Nai's daughter-in-law. Our minister, Rev Shen Wa Chin, thinks she must stay where she is for the time specified, 2 years and 2 months. He does not think anyone can meddle with their business. Her husband was a church member, too. The leaders meeting have not discussed the matter, but I presume they will excommunicate him. She had her faults, was a bold, cheeky girl and Mr Shen thinks inclined to loose living all along but she was quite a decent sort in the main. However, they say she was willing to go.
>
> It is an awful business, this pawning of wives. It seems to me much worse than merely selling off the one you don't want. The funny part of this do is that young Kao is fond of the girl and visits her often still. I suppose he was hard up; the family always is; chiefly because neither of the sons will work regularly.

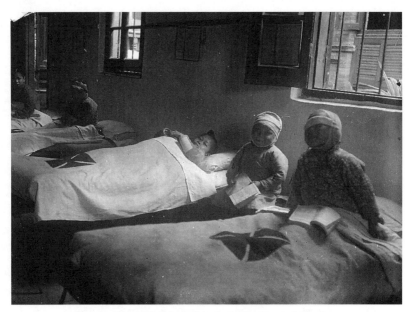

Some patients in Sally's ward in the Jubilee Hospital, Hankow.

Mr Shen says that inasmuch as Kao Nai Nai does not depend on her son for support and did not know of or allow this deal, that she is clear of all responsibility in the matter - all Chinese people will see that. I hope that is true. For it is a horrible business in a Bible woman's family.'

Sally goes on to talk about her hospital, which she says is full. A Mrs Lan has just given birth to a second daughter, without the sort of complications she had the first time round (fits) and a Mrs Wang has gone home after successfully averting a threatened miscarriage. Sally is full of concern for both young women and their husbands. Mr Wang is a Christian and she hopes Mrs Wang 'will follow her husband as a wife should, in any faith.'
There is news of a child who has lockjaw:

Our little boy with lockjaw is getting quite happy. He can part his teeth a little now but not enough to eat anything yet. He is getting fat, though, and laughs quite happily. He plays little games and enjoys himself and sometimes gives me a more or less military salute. They call it a "foreign salute." He is well on the road to recovery. That was robber's doing - shot the child in the row. Robbing here is often done with violence.

The letter ends with news of a Mrs Tan:

My friend, Mrs Tan, who learned her Bible stories so quickly, came back in the beginning of September. She did badly at first, but is better now. I think she came back to us because God wants her to learn more. She is getting on well with the doctrine. In fact, our present lot of patients are doing finely. We feel ever so hopeful about this. Sometimes no-one makes any headway at all. But these are great.

It was no doubt during her early days in the country that Sally was given the special job of being 'foot doctor.' Little Chinese girls used to have their feet bound from early childhood; it was seen as a sign of beauty in a woman if her

'Our little boy with lockjaw'

feet were tiny, albeit they were also hideously deformed, painful, probably infected and almost certainly nearly impossible to walk on. The practice began to die out after the Revolution of 1911 but, of course, did not go overnight and it lingered a long time in the country districts. The older generation of women would have been almost universally maimed by it. Sally once told a nephew how whole families of Chinese used to work in the rice fields and how the youngest child would be employed to move the grandmother's stool for her, so that she could sit at her work.

Sally had to go round the countryside unbinding these children's feet. She said it was a thankless task, for she knew that almost invariably, as soon as she had left, the child would have its feet bound up again, for girls with unbound feet were considered unmarriageable. To counter this, Sally used to visit the homes as often as she could. There is a photograph of Sally taken during these early years where she is holding a little girl on her knee whose feet have clearly been bound - indeed, it looks as if they have had to be amputated.

Other aspects of her life during this time are mentioned in a letter to her mother, Marion Wolfe, dated 4th October, 1918. The letter begins with an apology for having missed a week but she has been extra busy:

> I have a Sunday school class every week and had my prayer meeting to lead on the Monday and especially wanted to talk a bit to some of the children in the ward on Sunday afternoon.

The week had not been without incident:

> We had a rare old rumpus on Monday night. The first we heard was a bit of a scuffle on the lobby about 9 p.m., when Nora and I were thinking about settling down to read a bit. We usually have the nights from 9 o'clock on to do a little preparing or reading of some sort.
>
> We both went out and there were Pao and Hwa, our two senior girls, fighting. I did not take it in at first, nor did I recognise who they were. Hwa was in a corner near the door of the Ai Lion ward and Pao was on top of her, pounding her and both were abusing each other in terms that don't bear repetition.
>
> I got hold of Pao, the nearest to me, and when I had a hold of

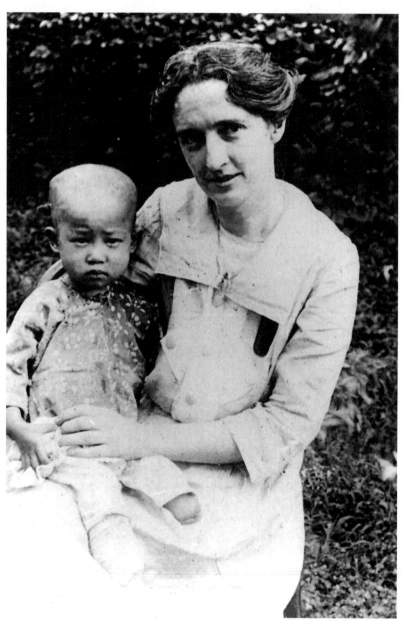

Sally with a little girl whose feet have been bound.

her two hands, Hwa kicked her. It was not quite fair really: but on the whole Hwa was far more knocked about in the scuffle than Pao. I could not help laughing, they were so angry and so silly: but it was really a serious business.

We got them along to Nora's study: they were still yelling. I said to Nora "You go along to the bedroom and find out what this is about." Of course, the nurses are in Nora's hands. I have nothing to do with them. She said "Do you think the others will say?" I said, "It seems to me you have got to find out."

So she said "Will you keep the girls here?" and went.

Whenever our girls quarrel, any of them, the first term of abuse they use is 'adulterous.' It is a vile word in a girl's mouth to apply to another… just because they are cross. This word was flying freely, so I told them they must not say it. I gave first one and then the other a bit of a shake and told them to stop it. They yelled and I suppose I did likewise, for Ethel heard us, right over in her house. She heard what Pao Ta Ku said, she did not hear my words, only that it was my voice.

My trouble was I wanted to be solemn and I could not help laughing. Pao Ta Ku, as usual, would not listen to anything I said. She never does, once she gets talking. I got Hwa Ta Ku to shut up, on the argument that all the patients and nurses had heard them already, there was no need to say anything over again for the benefit of the Chia family, who live under Nora's windows. She nodded her head, sat down in Nora's chair, on the arm of it, and cried a bit, so I left her. After a bit, I got Pao Tu Ku shut up, too, and I put her into my room and left her. I did not tell them they were to stay there, but they inferred it and did.

I went along to see how Nora was faring. I went to the bedroom door and met her coming out, having failed to get a word out of anyone. She said she would call in the minister. I hoped we could settle it ourselves. I said "Get them one by one and make them tell you. And get a note book and write down what they tell you. (Nora is sometimes apt to be a little inaccurate.) We discussed it for a bit and then she agreed. "Call Li Ta Ku first," she said.…

So I went into the bedroom, got Li Ta Ku up and sent her along to Nora in the nurses' sitting room…I stayed in the bedroom, and there was no talking there and no-one stirred except the ones I called up. Nora got through with the other nurses about 1.30 or so and I went to bed soon after. Nora had then to interview the two squabblers.

All evidence agreed that Pao Ta Ku abused Hwa Ta Ku at great length before Hwa Ta Ku began it all and also that Pao Ta Ku struck first. The girls all say Hwa Ta Ku had settled down to sleep when Pao woke her up to tell what she thought.

We have no end of complaints against Pao Ta Ku. Nora wants rid of her and so do I. But she asked Mr Shen [the minister] about it and he says don't. He says she and her family have bad tongues and will not scruple what they say and that Hwa Ta Ku could not stay in here if Pao Ta Ku left, her reputation would not stand it.

Mr Shen took a lot of trouble with these girls: he spent all yesterday afternoon talking to them and Hwa Ta Ku is willing to be moderately friendly but Pao Ta Ku won't.

… Nora is deeply depressed. Pao ignores her … she suggested betrothing her, before summer. Her father said he would consider it. If she was betrothed, we could dismiss her: but when she is not it is hardly fair, as her father could not keep her at home and no other hospital is likely to employ her and the only thing is to marry her right off to whoever turned up first. Hasty marriages are not apt to be a success.

Hwa Ta Ku apologised to Nora for the row…but as yet the other has not. And Nora is ramping because she caught her trying to intimidate the washer woman and make her say that Hwa Ta Ku said something to the effect that she would get Pao Ta Ku put out of this hospital before long…I have advised her not to allow Pao to lead prayers in the wards for a month or so, until we get a change of patients, as all the present lot know most of this row. It is Nora's business altogether and she must manage it. But she seems to look to me somehow and half say "What AM I to do?"…

… And we were hoping we were getting on a bit with our mission work. I guess we are too, and that is why the old devil is out just now.

On 31st August, 1919, Sally wrote to her brother William in Canada. The letter begins by congratulating him on becoming a J.P. It leads her to comment on the art of politeness, which, she says, seems to be the best way of settling the endless rows that arise among the nurses.

> ...'politeness' is classed as one of the cardinal virtues. And if we are sufficiently polite to the Chinese, young and old, men or women, we get them to do almost anything. On the other hand, 'foreigners' are not sufficiently up on the etiquette of the situation to be able to do the correct thing. I think it is [sic] 8000 rules there are in politeness. The extraordinary thing is the way it works, even a little of it.
>
> I came home a little cross one day, because my chairman made me bargain with a boatman, to get across the river. It is paid...[illegible...] and they always do it but that day they were cross and they would not. I told them they ought to. This was true. But they did not. When I came home, Hwa Tu Ku said "Why did you tell them they ought to?" I said, "Because they ought." "If you had said, 'I beseech you to do me a favour' they would have done it," she said. I suppose it was true. On the other hand, it is the only time they ever even suggested such a thing and it was done simply to be disagreeable: so it might have taken some time to get them round.
>
> And in dealing with young girls, I would much prefer that they should realise the rightness of a thing: and do it because it was right: rather than do it because I palaver them for an hour or two and finally request them to. It is not a sound basis. But it is Chinese...the mere mention of duty always starts the idea of other people's duties in their minds, to the complete exclusion of their own: or that the suggestion to a person's face that he might fail in doing his is so rude as to be quite inadmissible....

This letter to her brother was written from Kuling, which is 3,500 feet above sea level. Staff from the mission in Hankow and from the various foreign consulates and foreign firms often went there to escape the hottest weather. Kuling served the same sort of purpose as Simla did in India - a place of retreat where women and children, in particular, could go for the good of their health. They usually went from July to mid-September, thus avoiding the dangers of diseases such as malaria, cholera and dysentery, which were rife at that time of year.

Kuling was a lovely, cool place, with woods and tinkling streams and beautiful pagodas built out on distant mountain spurs. The place lacked such amenities as electricity and running water but had a church, a school, a hospital and a number of Chinese shops. People either went to their own private bungalows or, as in Sally's case, to a bungalow owned by their organisation. The missionaries had acquired a large plot of land in the 1890's for this purpose, though some missionaries had built their own bungalows, land being cheap.

It took a day to get there, going by boat up the river from the town of Kiukiang, followed by a walk to the base of the mountain and then a two-hour climb, either on foot or sitting in a bamboo chair carried by coolies. All the way up there were little booths selling Chinese tea where refreshment could be bought.

They went up to Kuling to escape extreme heat but could encounter bad weather while there, as Sally's letter explains:

> We are going down the hill tomorrow, if the road stands. There is a bit of a storm on. It was worst [sic] last week. Took the roof off one foreign house here. Broke the chimney off another (a new house, built this last winter) and punched it in through the roof and floor. With the result that the man and his wife and baby went into the cellar. The grown-ups were scratched a bit: but the baby was not hurt at all. He was sleeping in a cot at the foot of their bed and cot and all just went down. It is annoying, with a brand new house.
>
> But the damage in the Chinese quarters is worse. Two wealthy men, one reported to be earning about £4,000 a year (I state this because all the Chinese tell us it. His wealth being regarded as a reason why he should not be hurt) were killed, with their cook. The bit of hillside above their house subsided on top of them. The cook is little thought of: though he probably had a wife and family too. That two immensely wealthy [men] should be killed appals the public. (Do you remember the German note to Sir

Edward Grey, asking that the ship bringing Germans from India should have some distinguishing mark in order that it might be known and not submarined? It said 'The majority are better class people.' This is a similar idea).

Two bits of the hill road were washed away, in a great part of their width, on Thursday...one poor coolie is missing ...they planned an aerial railway from Lien Hwa Tong to Kuling. They surveyed the track: putting up red and white poles on the peaks ... they cut the brushwood... they gave the contractor Tls 3000 to get on with it. He is said to be Swiss Canadian. I hope he is not. Anyway, he and his Tls 3000 are missing. The money was Chinese and he is foreign: that is what is making us feel bad. Chinese have an idea that all foreigners are honest. This is nasty and awfully mean, too....

But I started out to tell you that I do not know whether I can have furlough next year or not. If not, I probably can in 1921. Miss Booth's mother is an invalid and not likely to live long. We are hoping to get Miss Oliver out to do matron for me: and we are hoping for another doctor...I am all right myself. Ever so happy now, except for a stiff back in damp weather....

Hare Ta Ku has lost the sight of that eye. But she is fine about it: she says The Grace of God is given her beyond measure and her days are peaceful. And that is true. She has been wonderfully sustained through what was a very painful illness: ending in blindness in that eye....

CHAPTER THREE

Troubled Times

In 1920 Sally was once more in the Jubilee Women's Hospital in Hankow. So far, her letters had revealed little of Chinese politics.

Yet China was in turmoil. A revolution in 1911, four years before she arrived, had resulted in the overthrow of the five-year-old Emperor, Pu Yi, and the end of the Manchu dynasty. After the revolution, a republic had been set up and the country was now nominally ruled by the nationalist republican party, the Kuomintang.

Hankow had suffered greatly during this revolution and much of it had been burned to the ground. It was soon rebuilt but then had to accommodate a great influx of refugees. By the time Sally arrived, the town would have recovered but the countryside at large would still have been unsettled.

Sun Yat-sen, a Christian, had founded the Kuomintang and had been elected President of the 'United Provinces of China' in 1913 but had resigned this position within a few months in order to try to unite the various rival claimants to power. These claimants were powerful warlords, heading vast armies, and the existence of these various rival factions meant that China was continually hovering on the edge of chaos during these years.

To make matters worse, Japan had ambitions in China. This led China to enter the First World War, declaring war on Germany in 1917, with the express purpose of preventing Japan from being granted German possessions in China in any post-war settlement. (Chinese troops did not fight in the First World War but 150,000 Chinese labourers went to France and were used to bury the dead, repair the trenches and build roads). Despite the fact that China had sided with the victors, Japan's interests in Shandong were recognised in the post-war treaties.

News of the treaty arrangements reached China on 4th May, 1919, and resulted in demonstrations, especially in Peking. Out of these demonstrations grew the May Fourth Movement which demanded further changes in the way China was governed. The May Fourth Movement was centred in Peking University and it soon took on a Marxist bias. Mao Tse-tung, who was a librarian at Peking University, got involved with these Marxist groups. In 1921, the Chinese Communist Party was founded, with Mao Tse-tung being one of its founder members.

Meanwhile, the Kuomintang continued to be nominally in control, ruling from Peking. At first they tried to make adjustments to accommodate the Communists but after 1925 the two parties came into ever greater conflict, a conflict the Communists eventually won two decades later.

In the early years, however, neither the Kuomintang nor the Communists were really in control. From 1920 to 1928 there was a series of factional wars going on all over China and it was warlords who had the influence, running vast areas of the country both in a military and in a civilian capacity. Each warlord was backed by an army and was usually in conflict with other warlords. Warlord armies were recruited from ex-bandits, the unemployed and the landless peasants and their existence wreaked havoc on local communities, from whom they exacted heavy taxes and carried out systematic looting to maintain themselves.

One of these warlords was Feng Yu-xiang. Like many of the others, he had risen to power from quite a modest background, having been a mere soldier in the regular Chinese army. He was unusual in that he was also a Christian and that he was keen on social issues as well as military ones. For instance, he tried to do something about the problem of opium smoking but was never based in any one area long enough to have much success with this. He also became famous in China for giving his troops a Christian baptism, *en masse*, using a fire hose.

Feng's army arrived in Hankow in 1920. This is what Sally had to say about it in a letter to her brother William in Canada on 3rd October, 1920:

We are all ever so delighted about our garrison. We have the

16th Mixed Brigade stationed outside Hankow, about 14,000 strong, under General Feng. It is wonderful. 4,500 are baptised Christians and lots of others are applying for baptism. Nearly all the officers are Christian. Of course, they know the General likes it. But it is genuine. China has never seen or heard of such an army. Everywhere, people are afraid of soldiers, afraid of their garrisons as much as their enemies. But without exception, wherever the 16th Mixed Brigade goes, the people are loud in their praise. They 'do violence to no man.' There are breaches of discipline, of course. Occasionally, a soldier is shot. But not often. And everybody knows it is the wish and intention of those in command that their men behave well. As Christian evidence, it is worth anything. The thing that nobody thought could happen.

All the men learn a trade, to practice in case of leaving the army. They obey their officers: they learn to read and write, most of them get Christian teaching. There are about 70 Bible classes everyday in the camp. The General requests the prayers of all Christians for these Bible classes. Some of our men go down sometimes to help. All of them are deeply impressed with the earnest tone of the camp. Mr Scholes was talking about it today. He says "In the history of Christian Missions in China, there has never been anything like it. It is wonderful."

Others also thought highly of General Feng. He was the only warlord to get aid from the Soviet Union, where his open attack on Imperialism in China and his genuine attempt to stop the Japanese advance in Manchuria was appreciated. The whole Chinese situation was so unpredictable and confusing that no foreign country backed any warlord for long but Feng continued to be a power to be reckoned with and in 1928 he helped the Kuomintang, led by Sun Yat-sen's successor, Chiang Kai-chek, to gain control of Nanking and to set up the National Government there.

The Communists, it appeared, had been sidestepped and after further years of conflict, Mao took his supporters off in 1934-36 on the Long March to the Hunan-xianxi border and there set up a successful communist state in Yunan. From here, young people were sent out all over China to spread his ideas. When the Japanese became a threat in Manchuria, the two sides,

Communist and Nationalist, joined together in an uneasy United Front to oppose the common enemy, going to war against the Japanese in 1937. Full civil war between the two groups broke out once more when the Second World War ended. The Communists won and Mao was in full control by 1949.

There were, therefore, four different phases of war during Sally's time in China - the warlord period, the Communists fighting the Nationalists, both Communists and Nationalists fighting the Japanese and then the Communists again fighting the Nationalists and this time succeeding in winning control.

Throughout it all, Sally worked calmly and sometimes incredibly bravely. Her later letters tell us something of the politics going on and reveal how much she had to endure and the wonderful way she set about it. In the early days, however, her letters mostly dwell on the work of the mission and the stress and the problems it and she experienced. Dr Pell, whom she mentions, was the Medical Superintendent of the whole Hankow hospital complex. In her later years (after 1928) this post was held by a Chinese.

Here is the continuation of the letter of 3rd October, 1920 to her brother William:

> Our mission is understaffed. Now I have had to send Miss Campbell to Kuling for 3 months. She is out of health and we are afraid of her getting something serious: getting thinner, paler, always tired. She was overworked and overburdened, of course. But to send her away, is to add to somebody else's responsibilities. It makes Dr Pell mad. He says it would be a good thing to shut up a lot of things and staff the rest decently. But he does not really think it. And it is not the fault of the Society. Naturally, with a call like there is here, people will try to do all they can. And they will no matter how many of them you send out. And the special stress now is the result of the war.
>
> Dr Pell supports me in sending Miss Campbell off. It is a big disappointment to her. But now I only regret I did not step in earlier. However, she may get on quite quickly... three months in the hills, doing only a little teaching or something, ought to do a lot for her.
>
> Mr Harker, of Wuchang, has just been ordered home. He is to

leave in December: nervous. The responsibility of guiding a big college of young men is great nowadays. They are all ramping patriotic and looking out for something to strike about and so forth. Our men have handled them well: better than any other mission in this centre. But Mr Harker is our 2nd nervous breakdown for that college in about 3 years. This leaves them shorthanded, as, of course, he is out of work now.

Today Dr Pell was summoned to Wuchang to see Rev Gadge, the Principal of Wesley College (Mr Harker is only a teacher there now, but was in charge until Mr Gadge got back from England. He has never been really fit since he was in charge of it). The cheerful question today is "Has Mr Gadge got typhoid?" Ailing a week etc etc. Mrs Gadge is pretty well and was to have had her second operation next Wednesday, unless this prevents it. I think I shall advise Dr Pell to go ahead with her operation in any case. But, of course, if Mr Gadge gets bad meantime, the anxiety of her operation won't help him. Great times.

I am thankful that I keep well. Also that I am just an ordinary member of the mission. I would not be like Mary Andrews for anything: I would rather go home. She has so many rights and statuses and things that she is a great nuisance. And our latest conclusion is that Miss Green, a newcomer, cannot be put anywhere but with Bertha and Mary, as otherwise Mary would be more than Bertha could stand. Miss Green [is] to be a partial protection. The deputation stationed Mary to live with poor old Bertha. So it must go on for a bit. But if Bertha gets to look much worse, I guess I shall have to step in there too.

[I do not know why Mary Andrews had such a special status. Presumably, Sally had written to her brother before about her and he understood what she was getting at.]

I lived with Mary in Kuling and know her and she is a general nuisance and cannot by any means be induced to stop talking. We all do a bit of talking occasionally but Mary does not seem able to stop…everybody thinks Bertha would break down if we took Miss Green away. I would not be Mary, not for anything. Nobody wants her anywhere.

The first doctor available is to go to Anlu, where Mrs Rowley's hospital wants help or will from the New Year, when Dr Cundall goes on furlough. They ask for "anyone", to do surgery for both hospitals. But they will not have Mary. It is a pitiable thing. And the joke of it is that she pities all of us, because we are only women and she has "the status of a man" and really thinks herself much better off than any of us.... Her attitude to the present situation makes me sorry she came out at all.

Nora has come back... [She] and I shall have this place to ourselves most of the time. She has been very decent so far...

... Aren't there a lot of furloughs coming on? It is to be hoped some of our folks that are in England get back and that we get some volunteers soon.

CHAPTER FOUR

The Children

A couple of years later Sally's life took a new course when she adopted her Chinese children.

A baby girl called Suteh was the first child she took on and I remember her telling me about her. How she was the daughter of one of the leaders of their Bible group who had died shortly after giving birth. The woman's husband had come to Sally and had begged her to take the child, saying he couldn't rear her. Because her mother had been so important to them, Sally agreed to care for the child herself. Girls were, in any case, of very little importance to the Chinese and were frequently left out on the hillsides to die or were married off as child brides. So that her future with her father would have been a doubtful one, had he been forced to take her.

In a letter dated 25th January, 1923 to some young cousins in Skibbereen, Fra, Harry, Avesia, Jim and Billy Wolfe, Sally commented on the surprise they must have got when their own new baby brother arrived and wrote:

> … You will be even more surprised to hear that I have got a baby too. Santa Claus brought her to me. And I am sending you a photograph of her. She is my very own little girl, a little cousin for Betty and Margery and you. She is called So-deh. And if you want to say it right you say So -teh——, like that. And that helps you to know that she is not meant to go in a cake.

Suteh 'all tied up like a parcel.' On the back of this photograph Sally has written 'Suteh in her christening dress aged nearly six weeks.'

This photograph was taken when she was six weeks old. Now she is nine weeks, and she can answer when you talk to her, and stand up straight in her bath. (She hates to sit down in it). She is ever so strong. But she is very thin. I guess your baby is bigger than her. When she was eight weeks old she was only seven and a quarter pounds. I weighed her once since, and then she was seven and three quarter pounds....

She came to me because her own mother went to heaven. And her daddy works on a railway, and often he does not come home in the nights. And he has nobody to mind Soteh for him. (I generally spell it Suteh, because people out here do)....

Don't you think it is funny to have a baby all tied up in a parcel, like this? I did. But it keeps them nice and warm and cosy. I used to call Suteh a little caddis-worm at first. But now she is too wide-awake to be like a caddis-worm. So I call her a fat lambkin. Now you know what she is like....

The letter ends:

> ...I will tell you a riddle that one of our little sick girls asked me one day. I think perhaps you can guess it. I did. It is "Their mother goes barefoot and so does their grandfather. There are a whole family of them, and none of them have heads or legs." And the answer is "Eggs"....

The second child she adopted, a boy called Johan, was, I understand, also the child of a Bible woman who died in childbirth. Sally must have taken him on very shortly after adopting Suteh, for in the photographs they look pretty much of an age and she talks of them in her letters as such.

Writing to her brother William and his wife Willie on 8th May 1932, congratulating them on the birth of their first daughter and sending the child a present of a quilt done in cross-stitch, Sally explains:

> All of us here use all the cross-stitch we can. There are lots of country women destitute and eager to do this (or any other work). So we have cross-stitched everything that can be done.

Johan in his christening dress.

She then refers to the time when her own children were tiny:

> You will have a great time now. I loved watching Suteh and Johan when they were wee. They were sweet. They slept in my room, and I slept outside on the verandah. One wet night I came in and slept on a camp bed. They woke up and saw me in bed. Neither could speak but their surprise was funny. I thought they had never before supposed that grown-ups went to bed at all. It looked that way. They told each other about it: and when Li Tia'i came in, they told her, obviously relating the biggest surprise they had had yet. And I lay there and talked to them and let them marvel.
>
> Another day, a cat came in and walked across the room, miaowing as she went. Later Suteh wanted to tell Li Tia'i. She opened her eyes wide and looked at the door by which the cat had come in, then she turned her head slowly towards the door by which the cat had gone out, following the cat's trail in imagination and saying "Aow, aow, aow". It was as plain as if she could talk.
>
> There isn't anything sweeter than a baby, unless it is two.

When they were a little bigger, Sally wrote about them to her sister Fan, who lived in Ireland and was the only member of her immediate family who had not emigrated to Canada. The letter is missing its first page, so cannot be accurately dated:

> A week ago I took Suteh and Johan for a walk, to see vegetable gardens. There are miles of vegetable gardens outside the city. I want the children to know all I can teach them about the work of the world.
>
> Suteh was the most communicative. Just before we left the vegetables, she stood still and, with a wee touch of awe in her voice, asked,
>
> "When it is dark, are all these vegetables still here?" "Yes," I said.
>
> My first vision was of all the little plants trotting in to the houses at dark: later I wondered whether she might suppose people collected them all up, every night, and set them out again in the

Sally holding Johan, with Suteh (seated).

morning. It may have been only theft she was thinking of.

Did I tell you another day I had them out in the same place, below the remains of the old city wall? It was a still afternoon, and the water in the moat was quite still. We stood behind it, and watched the reflection of the traffic on the base of the wall: a steady stream of foot travellers and rickshaws. The reflection was perfect. Then a horse and car came along. Johan tugged and tugged my hand.

"Oh, look," he said, in great excitement, "A horse and car came on the road and a horse and car came in the water." The coincidence thrilled him. Evidently, he had not got the idea before.

Three years later Sally added to her family, adopting a baby girl called Futeh. She writes about her on 25th July, 1926 in a letter sent to her brother-in-law, William Wolfe of Skibbereen:

I enclose photographs of the latest addition to my family, the babe with the ears that stick out and the soft little bendy bones. Some days I wonder what she will grow like, some days I think she is not too bad really, and there is nothing much to worry about. There is [sic] no rickets in this part of the world: and if she should go rickety, I think I would put her in the China Medical Journal, an honour which, however, I do not court for her. She is the best little mite alive, as happy as can be, and with a really charming smile.

If you think we live in a very palatial house, I will mention that that is the screen at the photographers…Suteh was a terror at the photographers. She would not keep still. It was a hot day; that is why my hair is all wet. It was not really weather for having photographs taken.

My children are very well so far. Suteh is a joy to see. She has a beautifully built little body, perfect everywhere. Johan is all right, but rather thin and lacking in endurance. He tires easily. The wee one is very different from them. I guess I was too quick in saying that she had not suffered from the famine that set her family wandering. She was breast fed and not thin; but she is not

Summer 1926
From left: Li Tai'i (the nurse) with Futeh on her knee, Johan, Suteh and Sally.
On the back of this photograph Sally has written 'Suteh does not really squint.'
Note Li Tai'i's bound feet and the top quality shoes Sally has given her children.

sound in bone yet. And it is all the more proof that her folks were not to blame in deserting her. What will happen this year, I don't know. I can't take any more children, anyway. Three is my limit. And we are in for another year of dire want mixed up with actual famine.

I believe God knows how to manage. But I wish there did not have to be famine and floods, pestilences and wars. But we'll come to the end of them some time.

This year there was a dearth of early rain and in many places people either were unable to plant rice at all or had it die after planting…so we prayed for rain. And, alas, the rain came, and flooded and ruined tremendous districts. At Paoching alone they report 5,000 drowned and houses beyond number destroyed. And it is so in many places and the crops all rotten or washed out. Even in Hankow many houses have a foot or so of water on the ground floor. My Johan is tremendously impressed. We have no water in our house, or even garden, but he sees it on the street. It has been so for a fortnight, but he has not got used to it. He is very graphic, and uses his hands to help make his point clear. He has a lovely little face for expressing wonder.

"You can't walk on the street," he says. "The water has come to here," pointing to his feet, as if he were still standing at the edge of it. "A lot of water", he says…"A lot of boats." He loves boats. The boats would, of course, be on the river. But he is not too precise.

I have told them the story of the 'The Three Little Kittens who lost their Mittens', only I said "stockings". Johan likes the tale and knows it perfectly. He tells it often, with the comment "I saw it" put in here and there. He means, of course, that he saw kittens and he saw new stockings for sale in the street and so forth. Suteh is less interested in the historic tale.

In hot weather, nobody does anything that does not need to be done urgently. So I am doing very little, except see the patients and fight with the ones who want to come in and I won't take them. It is too hot to crowd up, and the nurses won't stand it, and neither should I. And so we fight. I don't ever go to my little

Hway Chin Tiang Sunday School, partly because it is too hot, and partly because it would take 3-4 hours, and there is no-one responsible enough to be left in charge here that long.

As soon as the river falls a few feet, it will be better. But we can scarcely look for it to fall for another month. The snow water is coming down now. The trouble is that, with the river up, there is literally no drainage of the city: less than none. And that always brings dysentery, and often other things.

'I can't take any more; three is my limit' she says in this letter. The sort of tragedy she envisaged and the dilemma it posed were described vividly in a letter she wrote from Hankow to her brother William in Canada on 8th May, 1932:

We have two children here now that are just lovely. One is 3 or 4, the other a biggish baby. The mother got cholera very badly. It was days before she decided to live and even now she hardly eats anything and is still half stupid. Her husband was very nice to her; came to see her every day, bringing the two children. He was quite poor and yet he bought her a bun and a packet of Sun-maid raisins. She could not eat either, so he cried over that.

I took a few raisins and put them under her pillow, so she could get them if she wanted them: and told him to give the rest to the children, because the mother couldn't eat them anyway. He came three times: and the third time he got cholera so badly that he could not do anything. Dr Pell got him, and asked him about the children: he could only say their mother was in hospital. So Pell came for me to see what we could find out. We knew the children. So I asked a nurse to carry the baby to the women's side. (That lovely baby dislikes foreigners.) I told the three year old to go with him. And she did. Then I fetched her along to see her mother to get her identified. The woman knew the child. Then I sent them off to another ward.

That little girl has mild cholera herself. The babe is well. It is lovely to see the way the sister takes care of the baby. She feeds him and minds him as well as she could if she were twelve. They sleep on the same cot. And the babe is as good as gold when the sister is there, but cries if she is not. The only time the older one cried was one day she woke up and missed the baby. We are trying to make his mother go on nursing him (otherwise she will never raise him). And someone had taken him down for a feed. The little sister did not know where he was.

One evening it was time for mien (= a sort of vermicelli we give them for supper). A nurse gave them a bowl between them and it was not enough. The baby cried for more. I was busy in the ward at the time. The child held out her bowl and said,

"He wants more".

She did not fuss, merely waited a minute. Then she said, "There isn't any more," and settled the baby and herself down to sleep. Neither made any more bother. Later we got them another bowl, and the wee mite fed it to the baby just as well as anyone could. She did not taste it till the baby had enough. It was sweet to see. She mothers that babe all the time.

The father died. I don't know what they will do. Probably betroth the little girl and give her away.

Wholesale destitution is terrible to see. But some, at least, of the people retain their patience and their affections through it.

I wish that woman would hurry up and get well. They had some bits of things. We don't know anything about them. If she can't go out to claim them, they will soon be gone. She has sweet children, anyway.

You may like to see a few photographs of the house for destitute women and children that our folks are running at Hway Chin Tiang. It takes 500. Government relief gives rice only. We provide buildings, staff, etc, etc. Vegetables also are our affair. The government just gives the rice.

Margaret Swann is in it and several of our church folks.

They run a school for children, and one for women. Margaret gives the women what work she can get for them. We help with the sick. It is a good piece of work and well run. Margaret is good for that sort of thing. She lives with them and has a missionary job that anyone might envy. The school age is 7 - 70! It will last another month or two. We can get our expatriates in then, because there are some folks leaving all the time. Wheat harvest is on, and all that can go back to the country want to. If the country was at peace, all would go.

Alas, the rain is threatening to spoil the wheat. I wish it would clear up. If the wheat rots there is nothing but lawlessness and starvation everywhere. And the weather is cold and wet.

Cholera is terrible already. What it will be like in hot weather is terrible to think about.

In her letters dated 25th January, 1923, to her five little cousins in Skibbereen, Sally describes another child she was treating in her hospital:

Tell Mother that I was using the money she gave me for a girl called Shoo Jo Niang. She is a slave. Because where she lived there was no rain for ever so long. And first all the grass and the wheat got all withered up, and then the rice did not grow any heads of rice and so the people had nothing much to eat. Then they eat [sic] up everything there was, all sorts of things that I won't tell you about for fear you might play famines some time and get sick. Lots and lots of those people got sick. And then one day her daddy had nothing at all to give any of them to eat, so he sold Shoo Jo Niang to be a slave, so that he could have some money to buy things for the others to eat. She came a long, long way in a boat, and then somebody in Hankow bought her. But she was sick and would not eat anything. So they brought her to stay in our hospital.

You would think that after she had been very hungry for a long time she would like to eat things, wouldn't you? But she did not. She said, "First there was nothing to eat and now I don't want to eat anything."

We tried to take care of her. But for ages she would not eat anything to speak of, and she got thinner and thinner. I never saw anybody quite so thin.

Then she got awfully hungry and used to eat ever so much more than anybody else, and used to cry because she was always hungry, no matter how much she eat [sic]. So I had to stop giving her ordinary things altogether and now she only gets special things. Everyday she has one pint of new milk and some virol and some Benger's food that your money buys for her and some tinned milk and cod liver oil and an egg and some nice gruel that the hospital supplies for her. She is so thin I do not know whether she will ever get fat again. But now she does not feel hungry. And she hardly ever cries and she is beginning to talk again. Did you know that sometimes people get so sick that they won't even talk?…

Children with lockjaw, children suffering complications from having their feet bound, children ill with cholera and from malnutrition - Sally saw them all. She told a nephew she once even had a child brought into her hospital by its people that had been injured by a tiger. The child had been walking along a narrow path and had been knocked out of the way by the animal. She said the most terrible injuries could be inflicted by a tiger with just one single blow. So many children suffering with such a wide range of ailments brought to her and all so lovingly and expertly cared for by her. For, above all, Sally loved children.

CHAPTER FIVE

Living With Danger

Sally, we know, had several brushes with danger. The years from 1928 to 1937 are known as the Nanking Decade, when China was governed by Chiang Kai-shek and the Kuomintang. That government was weak and corrupt and was challenged by the Communists against whom a number of disastrous campaigns were mounted.

The Christian population and the foreign missionaries sided with Chiang Kai-shek, since his was the legitimate government. He was also favourable towards Christians and had himself been baptised into the Christian faith in 1930.

The Communists, however, followed Marx in condemning religion as being 'the opium of the people.' They also objected to the presence of foreigners in their country and this made them popular with many, for the behaviour of foreigners had often given offence. For instance, a park sign outside the International Settlement in Shanghai, which was mainly British, had earlier barred entrance 'to dogs or Chinese.' Anti-European feeling had culminated then in the Boxer Rising of 1900, when 186 missionaries alone had been murdered. Now the Communists were displaying a similar xenophobia, arguing that the continued presence of such foreigners gave China the status of a semi-colony. Foreign missionaries were included in this condemnation.

The civil war between the two sides began in earnest in 1927 when the Communists attacked Nanking, the centre of Chiang Kai-shek's government and took a cruel toll of the missionaries as well as residents. Hankow, well up river from Nanking, was that summer in the hands of one of Chiang's armies, under its commander Chang Fah-kuei. Half this army under the same commander later turned Communist and roved round China, executing capitalists at whim. It was this group that attacked Chungsiang in 1931, where Sally then was.

She wrote to her brother William on 19th October, 1931 from Hankow where, she says, she is 'back safely.'

> I was up in Chungsiang by myself for three months. Roads were too unsafe for Hadwen to get back: or for me to leave. We had rumours of all sorts and I had made certain preliminary preparations to leave hastily, should need arise. But that was all there was to it.
>
> On 1st October, soldiers began to dig trenches on the hill behind us: useless trenches, not suitable for military purposes. So we did not think much of that. I had various reasons to think trouble was brewing and various other reasons to think that it would not be for some days.
>
> Then on 2nd October, while I was serenely seeing outpatients, my servant came down hastily to say "Go away. They are firing on top of the hill" – i.e. a couple of hundred yards away. And as easily as anything I said "O, let them. The soldiers can defend all right." I was as sure of that as of anything. We had about 2,000 fully armed soldiers and a walled city and hills.
>
> For a moment I was for going on with my work. Then I thought I might do well to send the girls home. So I went to the women's hospital and told them all to go home. They began to collect their things and I scurried them out. If they were to go at all they must go at once. I got them on the move.
>
> And as I was coming back to the outpatient department I met Mr Chia and he said "You go away for a little while anyway." "All right," I said and went. Just as placidly as could be. I went and sat in the Wu's house. It is a big house and not rich. They are hospitable folks. They took the school children and me and the Chias and Shuys in and later four men nurses. I was utterly at ease there.

Then Miss Li said "There are too many people here. You come with me". So I did. They managed it well. I merely crossed two streets and went through another huge house to get to Li's place. A Chinese house has several courtyards in the inside of it. (I mean a big house has). The house I had to go through was on the slope. And as I went down an outdoor flight of steps in a courtyard, I paused and looked across at the hill. That was my first clue to the state of affairs. There should have been soldiers, flat on their tummies, defending that hill and there weren't any soldiers at all there, only people sightseeing. Then I understood. The soldiers did not mean to defend.

The red army halted a couple of hours to let the soldiers go into the city. Then they came on to the streets. Three quarters of the city and all the business is outside the wall. I think it was pre-arranged.

The red army numbered 7,000 or 8,000, [with] little equipment. They stayed two days. They killed Mr and Mrs Chia. They took four of our men nurses but released one next day. Since then I am thankful to say the other three have escaped. The reds fired the men's hospital and the girls' school. But the men's hospital folks put the hospital fire out. The girls' school is burnt.

They took all our theatre things and our most expensive and most useful drugs and money. They broke lots of doors and called local people in to finish the looting. They took everything portable out of our houses and bedding and so forth from the hospitals. They left the iron beds and big tables. They did not kill many people - perhaps 30 or so - but took a good many to hold for ransom. They never got into the walled city.

Several times red soldiers came into the Li's house but they never searched it, so did not see me. I hid near the front door, so could hear all that was said on the street and in the first courtyard. They were quite polite men, apologised for frightening the people etc etc.

They all left hastily on Sunday afternoon. I stayed on till Tuesday at Li's. On Tuesday a soldier of doubtful status called there and asked to search the house for stolen goods. (People were doing that all round). He did search, more or less, the front of the house. So I saw him plainly: but he did not see me. Then Mr Li stopped him. He said "Of course, you may search the house, if you have a warrant but I ask to see your warrant." The man said he had not brought it. So Li said "Go back and get it." He did not come again. But I had heard him ask for me. And they tell me he asked for me again inside.

I sent for Mr Chia, to say I wanted to go home. He and the second Li man agreed. The head of the house was out. It seemed to me that if the military were looking for me, for any purpose whatever, they were due to find me and I wanted to be found at home, to avoid implicating the Li's.

So I came home. Next day the soldiers searched the Li's house thoroughly.

But those days passed and the soldiers did not desert: though it was common talk that one third of them had planned to.

There were disturbing factors. I had very little clothes and no bedding and no money (same as everyone else.) Every night someone broke a hole somewhere in the compound wall. Every day a mason built it up for us. But I did not like it. There was very little that was portable in the place. It worried me. The third day I found that Hadwen's safe had not been opened. I felt better after that.

But anyway I was a little nervous every night. And when we heard that our whole garrison was leaving, I left too. It was not absolutely necessary but I did. There was only one road that was possible. It was long but we had to come that way: three days over land to Shasi and then wait for a boat down here. After the first day, the aspect of the country was that of peace. We got along quite nicely.

People are pretty friendly. I had no difficulty in borrowing money. And in the boat a lady absolutely insisted on my sharing her 'pai wo' i.e. a quilt thing. All passengers lay on the floor anyway. Everyone was nice to us.

And the folks fairly thrust things on me. I am set up in clothes already. They won't be gainsaid. Nell gave me two vests, Mrs

Rowley two combinations, Ethel a dress and a dress-length unmade, etc etc. I tell them I will soon have more than I lost! And I have money in the bank, don't worry about me. I am very well: have taken no hurt at all out of this.

Mr and Mrs Chia leave six little children, eldest 13, five eldest are girls. The reds meant to kill him: and probably would have managed it in any case. But he was betrayed by a young woman who really ought not to have done it. That is a pity. His wife threw her life away in a futile attempt to save him. They just shot her, in a bit of impatience. They held her one night and released her next day and made her go back to our compound. Then she went after them again and they say a man shoved her back nearly to our gate; but she followed them again: so a man shot her. It seems a pity. Chia was killed the first day. There was no sort of use in her fussing them the next day. However, that is what happened.

The two were very much attached to each other. Only it leaves six little children and not many relatives that can do much for them. Of course, the church will look after them, as a routine thing. (It was not for his Christianity he was killed: but because of his association with the Kuomingtang). He was a candidate for the ministry: the kiddies have the church support all right.

I don't know when we can get back to Chungsiang. Hankow is full of refugees from flooded areas and lawless areas. Mat huts by the thousand: and not too well managed, though lots of folks are helping. It is not easy to manage 50,000 refugees.

Harold Rattenbury mentions these same floods. He says they turned 'most of Wuchang and Hankow into one vast lake' but that the area where the Wesleyan Mission was housed remained above water.

There are two oral stories of other occasions when Sally was in extreme danger from either the Communists or the Japanese. They are not supported by written evidence and so are difficult to place. There was the time she and one of her nurses had to hide at the back of a filthy pigsty. Soldiers searching for them came and banged on the sides of the sty with sticks, then took a cursory look in at the door.

"Oh, this is too dirty even for pigs to live in," said one and they moved on.

It is quite likely the nurse was Hilda Shepherd and, if so, the incident would have happened during the civil war which broke out between the Nationalists and the Communists after 1945.

The other story has Sally being brought before a firing squad. Again, one must assume she was in Communist hands, though it is hard to say if that was in the 1930's or during the period after 1945. She told several people that her life was only saved by the intervention of one of the soldiers, who stepped forward and said she had tended him on some occasion (some versions say she had saved his life) and should therefore be spared.

Of course, had Sally been caught that time in 1931 in Chungsiang, she might not have been killed but she might have been held as some sort of hostage. Harold Rattenbury tells us that in 1934 two missionaries of the China Inland Mission were captured in Hunan. One, a Mr Hayman, was released after being held captive for 413 days and the other, Mr Bosshardt, was held for 560 days. Both were trailed round China by the Communists and Mr Bosshardt reckoned he must have covered 6,000 miles during his captivity.

Whatever the state of the country around her, Sally worked on unremittingly, dedicating herself to her patients. I am told that she said she used to work such long hours at the operating table that she had to ask two nurses working with her to straighten her up every now and again, so that she could keep going.

No wonder she became a legend in her own time. Harold Rattenbury, writing of the year 1934 about the Jubilee Hospital in Hankow in his book *China, My China*, has this to say of Sally:

> Each night, in my Hankow home, as I went upstairs to bed I could see the lights in the Women's Hospital opposite me; and almost always, on the stairs or passages, the shadowed figure of an Irish lady doctor moving about caring for some woman in her pain. When or how that doctor slept, I never could discover. She seemed to be on call at all hours of the day and night, and to hear her stories of the patients she had served made me feel that, if the sad and tragic side of Hankow's life were ever to be known,

there was the one person who could relate it. But why should she? Sufficient for her that one more day she had been able to help humanity in its sufferings. She knew and loved the people; grew early grey in their service; "stood like a rock in the day of trouble," as a Chinese colleague said of her. She was a Gold Medallist of Glasgow, [he is mistaken on this point - she never studied at Glasgow University], an able surgeon, and yet in her Irish way believed in ghosts and things. If you disputed or scorned, that was your ignorance, said this brilliant, sincere, straight and childlike woman.

He was right about Sally's belief in ghosts. She used to say all ghosts were well disposed towards humans and that no-one would ever be hurt by one.

Harold Rattenbury goes on to describe the Out-Patients Department at Hankow with its inscription carved in stone over the entrance:

'P'u Ngai I-Yuen' - 'The Hospital of Universal Love.'

He describes how, at the gate-keeper's lodge, the outpatients received a bamboo tally with a number painted on it, then went into the waiting room to await their turn. While waiting, a preacher read the scriptures to them from a preaching desk situated at one side of the room. There were five consulting rooms.

One of them was Dr Sally Wolfe's consulting room. There, he says:

… sits "the Lady of the Lamp", who never seems to sleep. She is examining women and children. Her hair is white. So they know she must be over seventy, though actually she isn't fifty. I could tell them why her hair is grey like that.

We know very little of what complicated operations she had to perform, what privations she suffered while doing them, how many lives she saved - because she never talked of it. We know she twice saved a girl from committing suicide because she told the story against herself. After the second attempt, as she came round, the girl looked at Sally and said: "Oh, God! You've saved me again!" "That was the only time I was ever called that," Sally would say, amused.

Then she used to talk about the time she delivered a baby which shortly afterwards went into convulsions. Sally was very puzzled. This was the woman's second baby. There had been no problems with the first and this second one looked normal enough. Then one of the nurses informed her that the mother had, in the meantime, become a heroin addict and they realised the baby was suffering from withdrawal symptoms.

Despite the troubled political scene of her years in China, Sally rarely alluded to actual politics in her letters. No doubt it was safer not to do so.

However, in a letter dated 19th February, 1933, written to her brother William, she does refer to the League of Nations delegation that visited China at the request of Chiang Kai-shek. The Japanese had engineered an incident in Manchuria which they then used as a pretext for overrunning the area. They thereupon established Pu Yi, the last Chinese emperor, as a puppet ruler of Manchuria, now renamed Manchukuo by the Japanese. China, as a member of the League of Nations, called upon that organisation for help and a commission was sent. The investigation was led by Lord Lytton. Sally's comments seem to suggest that one of the issues in question was whether the Japanese were running Manchuria better than the way the Kuomintang were governing the rest of China and that the wool was pulled over Lytton's eyes as to the real nature of the Kuomintang Government:

> Don't believe quite all Hope Simpson puts in the papers. He is gullible. I fear even Lord Lytton was taken in. ALL poor people were confined to their houses in Kenkiang and here, the days the commission was around. I suspect Wellington Koo goes along to point out that there are poorer people in Manchuria than any they saw here. These folks are accomplished liars. However, there are signs everywhere that the people won't stand much more from the Kuomingtang. We may get a representative government soon. People are taking heart again.

Wellington Koo was the Chinese envoy and Ambassador and had been educated in Shanghai by the American missionaries.

In fact, Lord Lytton's commission found against the Japanese but nothing was done to remove them from Northern China. They eventually went to war against the Chinese (killing, between 1937 and 1945, an estimated 10 million Chinese civilians) and Sally was later to find herself under Japanese rule.

When Sally did make political comments, they were more likely to be about events at home. She made brief but passing remarks about Ireland, referring to de Valera and the 1937 Constitution and his visit to London in 1938, remarks that reveal an anti-de Valera bias.

And in 1926, in a letter to her brother-in-law, William Wolfe of Skibbereen, she refers to the General Strike in England:

> What do you think of this coal strike? Perhaps I am too much out of things to understand but, as it looks from here, it looks as if the miners were utterly, inexcusably wrong and ought to be at work. England has done God's work pretty well for lots of countries besides England and I hate to think that any class of the community are heedless of the strength of the nation, because there is not a doubt that as a nation we lead in integrity and if you do, you ought to keep top. Bill's rule [her brother's] for railway travel is always get the best seat you can: you can easily give it up to anyone that you think ought to have it: but you can't get it for anyone if somebody else has it first.

Like everyone else, she was interested in the Abdication Crisis, involving King Edward VIII and Wallis Simpson and she wrote to her sister Fan about it on 12th May, 1937. Note, though, her unimpassioned tone, when so many people of her generation were vociferous in their condemnation of the situation. (Fan herself, for instance, held very strong views about the subject.)

> It is the coronation today. We sang the National Anthem, but that is all we did...I hope the King will do well and the Queen likewise. [George VI and Queen Elizabeth, the present Queen Mother]. Notwithstanding, I am sorry for our little Prince of Wales: even if he was getting a decent sort of wife - silly of him: and I think wicked of her. But I suppose they will get married now. And I wanted him to go on being King and chuck her, at least I did till this thing went too far.

CHAPTER SIX

Further Developments

There were several opportunities to go 'home.' She went on her first furlough from September 1921 to August 1922. She delivered her niece Marjorie while on this furlough, in Canada. She had what must surely be the rather unusual experience of delivering three of her nieces - her sister Fan's only child, Betty, in Ireland in 1912, Marjorie in 1922 and Sue, Marjorie's cousin, in 1927, during her second furlough.

Her third furlough was in 1934-35, her fourth in 1941. On her first three furloughs, she appears to have visited both Canada and Ireland. But in 1941, due to the war, she went only to Canada.

Her Chinese children, of course, stayed in China, looked after, I assume, by other missionaries.

On 19th February, 1933, writing to her brother William, from the Jubilee Hospital, Hankow, she says how much she is looking forward to seeing them all in Canada and describes an unusual problem:

> One little plan of mine has come to grief. Mr Chin, our Anlu evangelist, has a son about 18 years old. He is a difficult sort of boy. He learnt very little at school. I took him into hospital and he was rather good at night nursing but got muddled a bit by day. Last year we wanted Mr Chin to attend a Theological School for a term. And it seemed unsafe to leave that boy behind. So after much enquiry, I found that an American Mission School

would take him in. I paid for him and he studied there one term, without giving trouble and to some advantage. In mid-winter his father went back to Anlu. And before he left I asked him, and his son, and one other person whether his son ought to go back with him, or whether he should stay on at school. We thought he would do well to finish the year at school and get a certificate. So I sent his fees to a man I know, asking him to go and pay them in for me.

He says he accompanied the boy inside the school gate and then gave him the money to pay and left him.

But the lad went and bought a lot of things - 2 pillows, a blanket, a watch, some underwear etc and joined the army.

This seems a most disastrous move. Most Chinese armies are very undesirable and very undependable. They are always revolting or something. However, his friends went and got him out of the army. And they returned his purchases to me, including a military uniform! I have wired for his father.

It seems to me the first thing to do is to find out whether the boy really wants to join the army. If he does not, he had better go home. But if he does, his father had better look around and find out which regiment is best behaved, and see if he can get him into that: otherwise, he may just take the boy home and have him join up with the present Anlu garrison, which has quite a bad name.

Anyway, I am mainly responsible for the boy here. His father had better take over now. So I have telegraphed him to come down. This will be a big worry to him. He was well pleased that his son was at that school. I am afraid the appeal of the army is the idleness of the life. However, I don't know.

I asked a man to find out for me what that boy really wants to do. He says he has two choices; he would like to go to middle school or back to Anlu Hospital. Well - I meant him to go back to Anlu Hospital this autumn. That was what we were aiming at and he knew it. And as for middle school, if he wants to go to one, the absolute sine qua non is a primary school certificate which he has not got and which he was aiming to get this June.

71

That man said "He is too silly for anything" and it is about the truth. I hope he does not go to the devil.

Last year, Mr Kwan said that if he stayed at home without his father he would be pretty sure to turn bandit. I did not quite believe it then. But the transition from soldier to bandit is all too easy. Well, I hope we can do something with him: and I hope very much his father will get here soon. My most urgent fear is that when he does, the boy will have disappeared again. However, there are three good men, all friends of his father's, trying to look after him and he is not a bad boy, that even I knew, only silly and soft.

In her 1933 letter she writes about her adopted children:

Johan is quicker to learn that Suteh is. Perhaps that is as well. She can knit and embroider and wash the ware and sweep the house. She loves doing those things. She has just been to ask me for 40 cents to buy enough calico for two pillow cases, which she says she will embroider herself with "very pretty flowers." She does quite well with her embroidery. But she rather resents books. Still, she can read fairly well now. And Futeh, my little one, can knit beautifully. She will soon be six. They are all very well.

Five years later, in 1938, she wrote from Chungsiang to her brother-in-law in Ireland and asked him to send her Hall and Knights Elementary Arithmetic and Algebra:

If Hall & Knights are not in use, no doubt what the schools are using will do. I try to teach Suteh Arithmetic. And she is slow. She is one of those folks who want a "rule" for everything. Lately we have been doing things like "A man spent one fifth of his money and had eight dollars left. What had he to start with?" And for a change I wrote "A man bought 20 cents worth of peanuts and 5 cents worth of sweets and had 63 cents left. What had he to begin with? And she said "He spent 25 cents. And

Sally with her three children, from left: Johan, Futeh and Suteh.

then, bless me, she tried both multiplying and dividing 63 and 25. And, not finding either satisfactory, she told me she could not do it. So I said "Having 63 cents over, he could, if he wanted to, buy 63 cents worth of something else". "Yes," she said, "and then he would have spent 88 cents". "Yes," I said, "and that would have been all he had." O, she is dreadful. I wish I could get her to think.

But Johan was nearly as bad and he has got over it. But what we are doing now is what we did last year: which is not very encouraging. She has all sorts of stunts of her own. If I write,

$$7^1/_2 - 3^1/_3$$

she will as like as not work it like this

$$7\text{-}3 + {}^1/_2 + {}^1/_3$$

She has the serenest way for mixing '+' and '-' and '+' and 'x'. And once in a way she will turn a fraction upside down, all of which complicate things.

Yet a letter a year before, written in August 1937, had given this surprising news:

School examinations are queer things. All this past year I have been tusseling to get Suteh to know Arithmetic. She is almost unbelievably bad at it. I have got a little sense into her head, but not very much. She is bad at it, and there is no second opinion about that. But she took our connexional examination in June. And bless her, Arithmetic is her best mark! She failed in Chinese. Just one subject, passed in everything else and Arithmetic her crack subject! Yet still she will cheerfully shunt a decimal point a bit to the right or the left without any very obvious reason for so doing. And if I don't approve of it there, she will just put it anywhere else at random. And I have explained and explained…I have done every mortal thing I can think of to make her understand that there really is some meaning in the thing…there is no telling beforehand what sort of result she will get as the result of her calculations…and behold her with 78 per cent in Arithmetic!

They are allowed to make up one subject. So if she can pass a supplementary examination in Chinese in September, she may get the primary school certificate. I rather hope she will. She is so very keen on it. But she is not up to standard all the same. I don't know how they will place her in Hanyang. But I am sending her to that boarding school next term. She is a big girl now and knocks about a bit too much. And Mrs Chang, the lady who is supposed to be in charge of them, is not much good at directing or controlling them. And so I shall only have Futeh at home then.

In 1933 there was an enforced separation from her children, due to the fighting between the Communists and the Kuomintang. They were in Chungsiang and she was in Hankow. She wrote:

People say my little Johan is not at all well. I have tried to send him some Virol and Ostomalt. I hope he gets them.

Normally, however, the children lived with her, though at some stage Johan was sent away to boarding school. Once that happened, she tried to arrange her work schedule so that she would be around for his holidays. On 12th May, 1937 she wrote to her sister Fan:

I am planning to take a very early holiday this summer (12 May, 1937) and go to Kuling on the 10th June so as to be back here when Johan has holidays. Little beggar! He just won't write letters. I know very little about him since he left. But I think he is reasonably good and happy.

Then, in a letter in August of the same year:

Johan is home for holidays. He is little changed from what he used to be. He is as nice as ever. He has got a funny perverse way of refusing to do nearly anything I ask him to do. I don't see any

75

particular sense in it. But it does not vex me. He says, in effect, "I certainly won't". Says it with a smile, meaning "I will." And he goes off and does whatever it happens to be. He used to do it before he went away. He is little changed. He has scarcely grown at all, either. But he is fatter; the necks of his shirts were all too small this year.

Everyone else was away at Kuling and:

Yesterday, Suteh cut my hair for me. And Dr Tu's children were looking on. My hair is much finer and greyer than is usual here. Tu En looked at the little bits on the ground. "Imported hair" he said. Those two kids are great fun. They are ever so sweet. They spend at least half their waking hours in this house, playing with Futeh. She is much older than they are but they get along famously together.

In March 1938 she wrote from Chungsiang to her brother-in-law, William Wolfe of Skibbereen:

I came back here three weeks ago, getting permission from my doctors, on my promising not to attempt any work before the middle of March.

My knee is better. I hardly ever have pain in it now, and I get about pretty well on one crutch. I can take a few steps without a crutch at all. But I am very lame that way, much more so than with the crutch. I am pleased with my one-crutch gait lately.

I eat well and sleep well and am taking certain tonics and extras. Yet I doubt I am getting stronger. So I sometimes think of resigning in the summer. Six months is a reasonable time. If I am not pretty fit by then, I mean to resign.

But I hope I can stay on in China. The children are so terribly orphans if I leave them. The society would allow me a pension, enough to live on. And I have still got a bit of capital I could spend on the children....

I do not know what was the matter with her knee in 1938, nor why her arms were giving her such trouble in 1937 (see below). An entry in the publication 'Skibbereen Methodism 1798 - 1938' alludes to an illness but does not shed much light on it:

> Our Missionary,
>
> Amongst those from this circuit whom we most delight to honour is Dr Sarah Wolfe of Chungsiang, Hupeh, China, who has been for many years one of our most prominent Methodist medical missionaries. We all regretted to hear of her serious illness contracted while attending the wounded in Hankow, but are glad to know that she has now sufficiently recovered to be able to resume her duties.

Their informant was undoubtedly her brother-in-law, William Wolfe. Needless to say, she did not resign from her post in 1937 and in the end only left China when forced by circumstances to do so.

In the letter she wrote to her brother-in-law in 1938 she again refers to the children:

> Johan wanted to buy a football with your money. So I let him. He and I went together and bought it, when he was going back to school. It cost more than his share of the money. But I told him he must gradually repay the girls. I got for each of the girls a little leather attaché case. They love them. And they both still have money in hand, so they are all right meantime.
>
> Johan had wished for a ping pong table for years. So I asked a local carpenter to make us one. He took about a year to do it. But while I was away in Hankow it was delivered here. So Johan and Suteh played on it. And now Suteh, who never wanted to play ping pong at all, just loves it. She brings the school girls up sometimes. And sometimes I play with her. But as I have to stay standing where I am standing, she is too good for me. She really plays quite well now.

In this same letter, Sally tells of an unfortunate incident at the mission:

> I am the only foreigner here these times. Mrs Upton got terribly burnt about 9 weeks ago. Her clothes caught fire as she was feeding John by a fire in her bedroom. He kept saying "Ho. Ho" which is Chinese for fire: but she only thought he was commenting on having a fire in the bedroom. She was wearing a long Chinese gown, like we all do; with I don't know how many little Chinese buttons. Mine has 12. And they are very slow to open. When Upton came in he took her in his arms, out to the kitchen, which is ever so far away, and threw water on her. I don't think it was the best he could have done. He got his own hands badly burnt, too.
>
> He took her and John to Hankow the day after I got here. I took a car up, and they went down in it. It broke down three times with me: and with them it finally broke down and would not go. So the garage sent a car out to tow it. Mr and Mrs Upton and John still stayed in the original car. And coming into Hankow in the dark, it rolled off the embankment, head over heels, down. Fortunately it was not under its own power, or it might have blazed up. No one was hurt. John said the car was "tiao p'i" which is Chinese for 'perverse'. They got into Hankow after midnight. 17 hours on a bad road. Mrs Upton and John will hope to go to Hongkong, perhaps to England. Upton is due back here now. I expect him every day....

CHAPTER SEVEN

Increased Tensions

In 1932 the Japanese had invaded Manchuria and set up the puppet state of Manchukuo. At first they met with very little opposition from China, for Chiang Kai-shek appeased the Japanese, arguing that defeat of the Communists should be his first priority.

Many Chinese criticised him for this and in 1936, when Chiang flew to Xian to urge the troops there to put a greater effort into their fight against the Chinese Communist Party, the local commander went so far as to put Chiang under house arrest for not fighting to regain Manchuria. Eventually, however, Chiang Kai-shek was persuaded to join the Communists in a United Front against the Japanese. This led, in 1937, to open war breaking out between China and Japan (the Sino-Japanese War). The Japanese invaded China from the north and eventually controlled the land all along the coast and the lower Yangtse. Peking, Shanghai, Nanking (the capital) and other urban centres were occupied.

Appalling atrocities were committed by the Japanese in the process. People were buried alive in pits, put down wells, were shot out of hand and had their houses burnt. Huge civilian casualties were incurred in the bombarding of Shanghai in November 1937. Nanking fell after a fierce battle in December 1937 and 200,000 were massacred, a crime known as 'The Rape of Nanking'. Still the Japanese moved on - by June 1938, they had taken all Chiang Kai-shek's power base. Millions were homeless, thousands dead. The dykes of the Yellow River were broken in an attempt to stop them but to no avail and in the end Chiang withdrew into the hinterland, to Sechuan Province where he was followed by huge numbers of people. The struggle went on from there.

In May 1937, Sally was working at the Methodist General Hospital, Chungsiang and on 12th May, 1937, she was still able to write this in a letter to her sister Fan:

We are still as peaceful as can be here and all going well...

She goes on to describe a very normal existence:

... We have silkworms, I don't know how many, about 300. Everybody likes them: and it seems as everybody is keeping them in large numbers this year. It is fun to watch one shed his skin, and when he is halfway out, cast off his little face mask.

Last night we had a terrible thunderstorm. It blew down a long stretch of our garden wall, up near Dr Tu's house. I am afraid it did a lot of damage. Barley is ripe and can be reaped even if it is beaten down. But wheat is not ripe and will mildew and rot. It seems a great pity. Folks say bales of cloth were floating down river this morning and that can only mean boats capsized. Some houses were blown down too, not very far away. We had hardly any patients today: and this morning our registrar told us we should not have: that there was too widespread damage for folks to come.

We are now occupying the building the communists burnt down in 1931. Then it was the Girls' school, now it is our Women's Hospital. We have exchanged buildings with the school...

My arms are ever so much better, in fact I can pick mulberry leaves for the silkworms....

Just now Miss Li is running a fortnight's school for women: teaching Mark for beginners and Matthew to those who know Mark: also hymns, commandments, creed, etc. We have about 20 women most days. 1 - 4 p.m., no fee: but they pay for their books. I am responsible for teaching Matthew and the women are good. I feel every time, that they deserve better teaching than mine.

I wish the men's work was going as well as the women's. But somehow or other, it is not. Our minister seems to irritate folks, whereas our deaconess has just the opposite effect.

We have about 50 boys and 30 girls from the school in church every Sunday. That is very good, as the attendance of scholars is quite optional.

Everything is going well, only for that friction with the minister. I wish he could be moved quickly: but our chairman seems to prefer to shift nearly everybody else on the staff. It is to be our best master in the boys' school next: and I should like him to stay. However, the best thing would be if the differences could be got over. It is a funny thing. For our minister is a good man, only a bit rude to folks. So if you pray for us, pray courtesy for Rev Liu Hsih An. That seems to be our chief hitch. He is good.

Just now everybody is thinking about the war in the north. And naturally, everybody is upset about it. It was not unexpected. The Japanese have been aiming at it for some years. They got away with the Manchukueh affair, so now they are trying this. It is a shabby trick. They may have needed more room, that time, but Manchukueh gives them all the room they will want for a long time yet. This time it is not present need that prompts the move. Naturally, the Chinese feel badly about it. Most people want to fight, even if it be, as most fear it will be, a losing war.

Feng Yu Siang [the General Feng mentioned earlier] made a funeral speech for two of the generals that were killed a few days ago. In it, he said "You two, wait a bit. I am coming soon." That is about how half or more of the nation feels.

Just now the river is terribly high. Men are working for all they are worth to save the embankments. And it looks to be quite doubtful whether they can manage it. The river is still rising. It rose fourteen feet these last three days. We have had an earthquake (1st August) and wind and the weather is flood weather. It rains a bit most days, sometimes heavily, and long. We had not a summer like it since 1931.

I wish our mens' work was going as well as the woo somehow or other it is not. Our minister seems to irre... our deaconess has just the opposite effect.

We have about 50 boys + 30 girls from the school in the day. Our Sunday morning congregation is as big as the church, every Sunday. That is very good, as the attendance of... quite optional.

Everything is going well, only for that friction with... I wish he could be moved quickly: but our... seems to prefer to shift nearly everybody else in it. It is to be our best master in the boys' school, + I should... to stay. However, the best thing would be if the diff... got over. It is a funny thing. For our minister is o... only a lit rude to folks. So if you pray for us,... courtesy for Rev Liu Hsil Aw. That seems to be our... ...d. He is good.

Your loving sister
Sally.

Sally's neat hand: portion of letter to Fan dated 12th May, 1937.

Just now they brought us a lying-in woman, from a house on one of our streets, because they have got two feet of water in their house.

I have sung my throat out, teaching a few patients to sing "Joy, joy, joy, with joy my heart is ringing." And I am not a bit too good at keeping the tune myself! They, however, are quite keen on it, so I have promised to complete their education on that particular tomorrow. We began with the nobleman's son who was sick at Capernaum, and went on [to] the chorus, which they learnt very well. I ought to do more with the teaching of patients; It is awfully hot certainly, but no hotter than doing anything else.

Mr Hsu, our hospital evangelist, has left us. Left in a bad temper too, unfortunately. And on the way home his only child got dysentery. They took her to Hankow, but she died, as nearly all babies do, with dysentery. That is pretty hard luck; And we have no evangelist now.

Our church is at sixes and sevens, too. But perhaps we are a little more amicable than we were a few months ago.

The others are still in Kuling. I took my holidays very early so as to be here with Johan. So I have the place to myself this month.

Writing from Chungsiang to her brother-in-law William Wolfe, in March 1938, she relates what had happened over the friction with the minister:

We have an unfortunate bit of jealousy here. The minister's wife has taken a notion the deaconess used to see too much of the minister. So now they scarcely speak to each other. I paid the deaconess's salary last month, because the minister was afraid of his wife, to do it himself. A most unreasonable jealousy. The minister and his wife are 54, and the deaconess is about 40. And they are all good people. And between the deaconess who is an aristocrat, and the minister, who is a farmer, there is a wide gap of social distinction. As a case of jealousy, it seems to me to lack foundation. Yet it is very unfortunate.

And she again mentions the war:

> Most people think Hankow is pretty safe for a few months yet,
> except, of course, from air raids. But lately [the] Japanese have
> only been bombing the airfields and arsenal. So the general public
> takes little notice. There are a few folks killed in every raid. But
> very few. After that one bad raid on Hankow and Hanyang, the
> Japanese have been very good about that.

In December 1938, though, the war was much closer. She writes to Fan:

> I fear this letter will be a long time getting to you: but yet I guess
> it will arrive sometime. The Chinese post-office seems to manage
> to get letters to their destination, no matter what obstacles it has
> to overcome. We often marvel at its efficiency.
>
> We are getting along fairly normally here. We had one alarm, a
> week after the Japanese came into Hankow. It then seemed as if
> they were pushing on in this direction and making some way,
> too.
>
> Nobody wants to be caught in a battle, if he can keep out of it.
> So this city decided to move out. Some people really went away:
> but most only moved off into the surrounding countryside and
> hills, to be out of any actual battle and to come back again
> anyhow, as soon as they could.
>
> Our schools and hospital went off, too. Rev R. L. Upton and
> Tom Richardson constituted themselves gatekeepers, day and
> night. They locked the gate at 5 p.m., every day. But one of
> them and a servant always slept by the gate at night. We built up
> three other gates.
>
> We had about a hundred refugees here. By day Miss Li and I
> dressed wounded soldiers, dressed them and gave them a dressing
> to put on next day and sent them off. We had no one to take care
> of inpatients; and anyway, in those days, we should not have
> admitted soldiers. For if the Japanese did come, they would
> probably shoot them: as they have done elsewhere.

That panic passed in a week or two, and since then we have been getting along nicely. The hospital has only about 30 patients now: but we are preparing to open another ward, that can take 20 more. Some days we see 80 -100 outpatients. And the schools are running on an abbreviated schedule.

The opportunities of evangelistic work are great. And I am ever so glad the schools have started up. Because till they did, I had to put in some time looking after the children.

We have lots of Chinese church wardens on the compound: people from various places, refugeeing here, both men and women.

But for a while a strange inertia settled down on everyone. Upton and I worked hard to overcome it. I daresay Richardson did too: but I don't know. He is a visitor here: sent to keep Upton company. For in these terrible times one foreigner would have an almost intolerable burden to bear. It is better with two.

We are afraid things may have gone badly in Wusueh: no news for four months, which seems to imply that the news is the sort the Japanese do not care to publish. Anyway, I guess Hadwen and Hancock did all they could. And if they are dead, as I think likely, how can a man die better? As Horatius is reported to have asked. We know nothing. I only guess they are dead, because we have not heard.

Upton is doing very well here. I feel rather proud of him sometimes.

We don't see far ahead these times. But God can.

Of course, distress is widespread, and often acute: and of course, money is hard to come by, since we are cut off from Hankow. But food is plentiful and cheap, so far, all except salt and oil.

I am glad we got back from Kuling. I was beginning to think I was no use, and then circumstances give me a chance like this! And I am well. It is lovely to be here. And we only just made it. Nineteen days we were here, when that panic came on, and all the hospital staff left, except Miss Li and myself.

I suppose if the Japanese do come here, the same will happen again. Anyway, it is quite evident that Upton, Richardson and I stay here whatever happens, so we are at rest here.

Barring accidents we should be safe here. It would be outrageously bad bombing to hit us. They could scarcely do it and claim it was an accident. We fly three flags all the time, and have three big ground flags too, painted on wood, for observation planes to see. They don't really count for bombers, as they don't see them till they are overhead. There have not been any planes about lately.

We have twice heard from Hankow and twice from Sui Hsien.

Johan has just had jaundice but he is nearly over it now. In fact he is quite well, only that he still looks a wee bit yellow.

Malaria is rampant, and quinine running very short. Fortunately Dr Tu had bought in all the drugs he could. But seeing 400 - 500 outpatients a week, etc, etc eats up your stocks.

I am hardly lame at all now and am strong again, stronger that I had thought I should ever be again. Kuling is a great place.

You would admire the Chinese if you saw them these days, so patient, so moderate, so good about everything. I guess God is proud of them. Anyway, I am.

Sally surmised that Hadwen and Hancock were dead but Fan scribbled the words 'We heard they were safe' in the margin of the letter sometime afterwards.

It is interesting to read that Sally put some time in looking after the school children. We know that she acted rather as Gladys Aylward did, when the latter led over a hundred children in 1938 across the mountains in Northern China in order to escape from the Japanese. Sally never had to put her plans into action but she did take a group of children out every day for long walks over difficult terrain, training them in case they would need to flee on foot.

Some time between 1938 and 1941, the Japanese did arrive at her hospital and demanded to search it for wounded soldiers. She refused to allow the soldiers in unless they left their guns at the door but they replied that their weapons would be stolen if they did that. She then told them that no-one would steal anything if she stood guard over them and, incredible as it may seem, they bowed to her will and left her in charge of all their firearms while they carried out their search. Presumably there were no Chinese soldiers in the hospital or she wouldn't have let them search at all and the letter quoted above clearly indicates she always tried to treat the Chinese soldiers at once and then send them on their way. It was a 'Catch 22' situation, for in later years she told people that treating bandits' wounds was tricky, since "You felt that your own safety depended on the outcome of your work".

She told a nephew that the Japanese were more of a nuisance than anything else, demanding to have their photographs taken with the staff and there is a photograph of her standing with two such soldiers. One of Sally's letters to her Canadian relatives came in an envelope which had the following written on the bottom left-hand corner:

'Per courtesy of an Officer of the Japanese Imperial Army.'

However, the letter that came in it got divorced from its envelope and since the postmark is in Chinese script, we do not know when that favour was done.

It seems that the Japanese eventually cleared the missionaries out of Chungsiang, for a colleague, Nancy Yates, recalls Sally arriving from some 'up country station' at the camp at Wi Shen Miao where she was being held. This is how she remembers Sally's arrival:

One day a lorry full of Japanese soldiers arrived, with Sally in her Chinese gown and woollie cap perched atop the pile of soldiers' luggage. Next morning was our prayer meeting and she was to lead it.

This is how Nancy Yates remembers Sally's address to the prayer meeting:

She spoke on 'The always perfect and acceptable Will of God'. She said we all obeyed the will of God but often grudgingly. Then she told us about a case she was called to inside the city and not long before curfew. (When the gates were all locked and no one on the street but soldiers). The house was freezing cold. When Sally asked them to light a charcoal fire to warm the air so she could uncover and examine the young mother and heat some

Sally posing with Japanese soldiers, at the hospital's main entrance.

water and boil some instruments etc, the women burst into tears, the young mother was in such agony all day they hadn't been able to leave her. When the man of the house came, they sent him for firewood or charcoal and all the men who sold it had sold out already, nor would the neighbours spare any of theirs. Someone said Dr Wolfe could deliver babies when everyone else failed. So they sent for her.

Sally just prayed aloud in Chinese and asked the Lord to send firewood. While she was praying, there was a banging on the door. Was it a soldier to tell them their lights should be out? No. It was a coolie with both his baskets full of firewood!! He had spent all day and sold nothing, the gates were shut and he couldn't even get through their secret way of escape without losing his whole load. He saw a house with a light still on. He was desperate to sell some before he climbed up the wall and squeezed through the secret tiny gap and went home.

So the coolie stayed whilst they cooked up a good meal and Sally delivered a lovely baby and then when all was cleaned up and everyone rejoicing, they wanted to hear how God loved them and He died for them and it was His perfect and acceptable Will, to bring them to know and trust Him and forgive all the their sins and guilt etc.

What Sally experienced in the camp at Wu Shen Miao was, no doubt, a form of 'house arrest'. She was lucky that she went on furlough in 1941 and so missed the worst of the Japanese occupation, for after the second half of 1942 people such as her were labelled 'enemy aliens' and were interned in prison camps.

Had she stayed on in China, Sally would probably have been interned in Shanghai. Those who were interned there (business people and others as well as missionaries) were not released until the end of the war in 1945. Ethel Wagstaff, the evangelist whose missionary career in China had begun at the same time and place as Sally's and who is mentioned in one of her earliest letters, was one of those who suffered in this way.

CHAPTER EIGHT

An Enforced Break

During her 1941 furlough, Sally's life changed again. The next letter that has survived is dated 3rd March, 1941 and is written from the *S.S. President Coolidge*, nearing Honolulu. It was sent to Fan and William Wolfe of Skibbereen.

As you may see, I am going home and my next letter will probably be from Elk Point. [In Canada - the home of her brother William].

This is a big boat, luxurious. I am travelling 3rd class, with "tourist privileges" i.e. the right to walk 2nd class decks and come to 2nd class meals and I am regretting the "tourist privileges," because plain 3rd class would have done quite well enough and been a lot cheaper for the Missionary Society.

We have 8 people in our cabin and most cabins are the same, also most are quite full. I brought my own wash bowl and am glad I did. Because we have only one wash bowl in the cabin and everyone uses it, for washing stockings etc etc, as well as faces and hands. However, I use it for clothes-washing too, same as the rest do: and I have my own for my face and hands. The beds are good enough, only they have no rims and no curtains.

We had calm weather at first: then two rough days. One night we all stayed awake all night, to keep from falling out of bed!

That evening I fell off a sofa. It was funny. They had tied up the extra tables and chairs to a big central pillar, also they tied sofas and chairs round the walls. Another lady and I were sitting on a wall sofa and when the ship rolled, it began to slide, then its rope stopped it suddenly. Both of us tried to lean our feet on the floor, but it was polished linoleum, and it just fell away from us, so we skidded halfway across the floor and finished up among the legs of tables and chairs in the middle of the room. Two gentlemen came to my assistance. I was not hurt at all. The other lady was younger, so no-one came to her immediate assistance and she skidded back again, quite unhurt! It was ever so funny really.

But the poor piano had a bad time. They had tied it by the legs and it wrenched itself right off one leg, and then fell over. So the men made a quick scoop down on a bunch of children, to get them out of the way, before that piano took to waltzing round. It was quite sensible of the men, and exactly what you would want them to do: but it frightened one little boy so badly that he cried and cried and was afraid of being drowned. I don't know how long it took his folks to get him anyway sensible after it.

So we all went to bed and lay awake, trying to stay there, while our trunks kept slipping from one side of the room to the other. No water came into our cabin but the alleyways were swilling for a bit and some 3rd class got it in their cabins too. About four or five waves broke in before they got the watertight doors tight. They shut them after the 2nd wave, but did not seem to think of screwing them up tight, so every wave sent a fair lot of water down. Americans are not so capable about ships as Europeans. An officer came down, cross. "What do you call this, anyway?" he said, "A swimming pool?"

At table and in the pantries, they broke a horrible lot of crockery, crack after crash, horrible to listen to, and quite unnecessary. Some passengers said "Government subsidised" but I thought it was just straight incompetence. The second day they did much better. But it can't have been the first time they ran into a bit of a storm, and it was not a bad storm anyhow.

And another funny thing is, I was not sick at all, I that sometimes go sick ashore. I am ever so delighted about not being sick. I think it comes of spending three weeks in Shanghai first, also getting two calm days to begin with.

I do not expect to come to England or Ireland this time. But I greatly hope I may be able to return to China. The children are too young to leave yet. It is two and one third years since I saw Johan. Poor little fellow, all off by himself all this time. He is doing well at school, and writes happily, in as far as anyone can be happy these times. The girls are not doing too well at school, and indeed their school is a make-shift affair, since the Japanese occupation.

I wish I could do better for them, but I can't. War hits everybody, and you can't expect it to pass your folks. Suteh is betrothed. But her man is hurt by the war conditions too, can't finish his training as we would wish. Suteh is going to our mission hospital at Shihweiyao to take nursing training. Miriam Driver is matron and I have thought it the best arrangement to make for Suteh. Suteh has been studying well, and is getting on quite satisfactorily at school, only she is years behind girls of her age, poor girl. Futeh is a clever little girl, and ought to be getting on well, would if I had her by me. But every report I get from school says she is lazy and won't study. I don't altogether blame her, given better conditions she would do better. But I can't get better conditions for her, so she has just got to do the best she can with what there are, and I have tried and tried to explain that to her. She is a nice kiddie anyway. All my three are nice.

Chungsiang is in the fighting again since I left. Two and a half years at the actual front for that one poor town. However Dr Tu and Dr Oertell and Rev A. P. Hadwen are there. And Dr Oertell can do more than I can now. So I am not sorry to be away.

Sally's next letters to Fan are all from Canada and one, dated 31 October 1941, contains interesting insights into her thoughts, as well as family news:

… I have just got your letter telling me of Bridgie Walsh's death.

I guess the older folks are all for slipping away now. We ourselves aren't so young any more. Sometimes I think it seems quite funny that we should be so old…

…The news from the Pacific does not sound very good these times. Can I get back to China in the spring? I think it partly depends on whether the Germans get Moscow or not. Japanese [sic] sit on the fence at present, or so I think.…

On 18th March, 1942 she appeals to Fan and William Wolfe:

Please lend me £20.0.0. It is cool of me to ask it. But war time regulations prohibit shifting money. I have been trying and trying to send some to my Johan. He wrote that rice was 100 times its usual peacetime price, and other things also very dear. In consequence of this the money I had left for him was all used up. Well, there was a difficulty. I wrote to Rev. Clifford Cook, at Changsha, asking him to lend me some, or borrow for me. The letter was returned to me, undeliverable. I had money in Hankow: if only I could get at it. I have been thinking and trying all sorts of ways possible. Some folks want to send money one way and some the other, and once in a way you can arrange it, on account without actual transfer of money. We have been doing this sort of thing across the Sino-Japanese fighting front for long enough. I want to send money to Johan, but can't. A man in Syechuan [sic] wants to send money to his wife in Hupeh but can't do it. We arrange that he pays it to Johan, and I give the equivalent to the wife. It helps both families, and is within wartime regulations. No money crosses the frontier. Well, this is the same sort of thing. I now owe Miss Hilda Porter [of the Methodist Missionary Society] £10.0.0., for Johan. But I am asking you to send her £20.0.0. for me. So that if she can manage another £10.0.0. some other time she may have it in hand. When we get peace, I will settle with you. I cannot do anything about it now. Assuming that you will oblige, many thanks…

…I have come to work in a small hospital here. But, as yet, I am only corresponding about my registration. Every province has its own laws. I think I can get registered. But till I do, my position here is a bit uncertain. Canada is short of doctors. I could register in Alberta or Ontario: whether or not in Saskatchewan, I don't know.

Smeaton is a nice little town, not unlike Elk Point. There are, however, more trees near the town. Snow is deep about. There are lots of spruce trees near the hospital. It is very pretty...

...The war news is just awful, isn't it? The Pacific zone of it anyway....

On 29th May, 1942 she wrote again to Fan from Smeaton:

Uncle Frank [a doctor in England] got a certificate that my name is on the British Medical Register. And on that, the College of Physicians and Surgeons of Saskatchewan has at last granted me a permit to practise in Smeaton and its vicinity...

...The Mission House continues to urge me to return to China now. I am trying to get a permit to leave Canada, in the hope that a passage may turn up. So far I have not got that permit. But I have just got my passport renewed for a further period of two years. It is not a bit easy to travel in wartime.

I like being here. If I was not due elsewhere, I could settle down here all right. The people are friendly and the place is pretty. I am almost too old to take up work in a new country. Conditions here are about as different from what I am used to as they could be. Fancy, we have only two nurses, one for day duty and one for night! We have a matron too. But she does nothing at all, not even helping with an accident. I don't think I ever had less than 16 nurses before. And also I had got used to having a house surgeon. Once I had three of them. Well, I am sure it is good for me. And I like it quite well.

At the thaw the roads were terribly soft. Cars and trucks used to stick and had to get tractors or horses to pull them out. I have been stuck in the mud often. And, because I look so old, people don't like to let me walk. But you can get through lots of places on foot, where you can't in cars or trucks...

...I have put in a vegetable garden: potatoes: peas: carrots: parsnips: radishes: vegetable marrows: cucumbers: beets: lettuce: corn: and strawberries....

Writing to her brother William in Elk Point, Alberta on 11th July, 1942:

We are fixing up our chicken-house for a mortuary. We have got a floor put in it. That was my idea. And the Board fell for it at once. It is just dreadful having a hospital of only two wards (it really has three, but I now occupy one) and no mortuary. Also it is annoying to have chickens scratching up everything you set in your garden. And for what eggs we were getting it was not worth while....

I have not yet heard that my permit to practise has been "finally ratified". But I think it has.

Yesterday, I got a document "On His Majesty's Service" directing me to form a board of three, myself and two others, one to be a doctor if I can find one, otherwise two businessmen, and report on the employability and capacity for wage-earning of a man who lives twenty miles from here, at Choiceland. I know nothing about the Choiceland people. So I mean to go an [sic] see our policeman about that, if he is at home today. We have a mounted policeman here, and he ranges over a wide area, which I believe includes Choiceland.

And again to Fan on 12th July, 1942:

This is a photograph of our hospital. Did you ever think it could really be so small? But it is a nice little place. And it serves the community well.

Of course, there are lots of inconveniences. For one thing, I have no consulting room: and no waiting room for patients. They sit in the hall. Also there are just three wards. One has 4 beds, the others 2 each. We have also one cot for a child, in a two-bed ward: and 4 wee cribs for babies. (Half our work is maternity.) Since I came here I occupy a two-bed ward. And that leaves us just 6 beds, in 2 wards. Well, it is easy to see that that is not convenient.

I should never have thought of it. But one of our hospital board members suggested that I should buy a house. And when we priced it it was $300. So I said "No". And two other members of the board said, "We know a house that would suit you. And it is only $150".

So then I began to sit up and take notice. And the result is as stated.

The mission has agreed to pay $10 a month rent, for an office for me. So now I expect they will pay me $10 a month rent for this house. If so, it will ultimately become theirs, when they have paid off what it costs me. If I leave soon, I may lose out on it. But if I stay a while, the investment should be profitable to the mission. And, as I say, it is fun: makes me feel … O, I don't know how it makes me feel. But I like it. I have bought a second hand armchair for $5 too. I have hardly bought any new clothes since I came to Canada: and don't intend to. But Kitty and Tom Johnson [her sister and brother-in-law] gave me a lovely winter coat, at Christmas. I could have done without it all right. But it is warmer than anything I had. What I mean is, I really am being loyal and not spending money unnecessarily.

We have a nice potato patch. The nurses helped seed it. I did all the earthing. And it looks very nice. Mosquitoes are FEROCIOUS this year. I rub myself with wintergreen oil or… other preparations. It helps. But the mosquitoes are not long deterred by any device I have yet discovered.

The rest of my garden is not very good, largely for want of care. The potatoes took a fortnight to earth, and meantime weeds grew elsewhere but worms are pretty bad too. And I have had other adventures.

I put in a row of cucumbers. They came up well. Then I had to shift them all, because they were just over a drain pipe that needed attention. Never mind. The weather is wet. They stood the transplanting. The dog elects to sleep on my pansy bed. And I hauled the earth to make it, in a kiddie car. I think it was 14 loads. And my best radishes, really promising ones, are just where my newly acquired house will be hauled over them. These are some of the vicissitudes of my gardening....

Tom Johnson used to tease Kitty and me for playing with a hose they have for watering the garden. He used to say we raced for it. This year he "beseeches" me to come back and beat Kitty to it sometimes, so he can get some dinner sometimes... a hose, that runs freely, on its own, is rather fun to play with sometimes, don't you think?

You will let me know directly you hear from Betty, won't you? And it does not seem so long since that little summer baby came to you at Glandore, does it? And Willie was horrified at my suggesting that we should bring her in by the kitchen door. "Gracious" as Maggie [a maid] once said, appropriately "Isn't it a fright how they change?"

Another letter to Fan from Smeaton on 30th August, 1942 congratulates her on becoming a grandmother:

I was very glad to get your letter telling me that I really am a grand-aunt, and you a grandmother. Congratulations. Is Willie properly proud? How time flies...

I am settling down here. I do not mean to stay, if I can get to China. But meantime I am settling down.

I guess I told you I bought a house, didn't I? I gave $150 for it. And it is costing nearly as much more to fix it up.

It was a butcher's shop: and after that, the butcher used it to store hides etc in. "Not nice" you are thinking. And you are right. We ventilated it, and scrubbed it twice. And still it smelled strongly of stale hides. Then I washed it over twice with permanganate of potash solution. That stained the floor a nice dark brown, and reduced the reminiscent smell considerably. Then I put on three coats of varnish. And the very first stopped the smell. There is no smell about the house now. In fact, the house is lovely. I nearly said it is a little dear. Then I perceived that that statement was open to misrepresentation.... At first it

Fan and Willie Wolfe with Betty, the author's mother.

swung a sign 'Meat Market'. I have taken that down.

Yesterday I finished varnishing the bedroom floor. O, I forgot to say the bedroom floor is all new: also the ceiling. There was no ceiling. I have been sleeping in the bedroom for about a fortnight. We needed the ward I was using in hospital. So I moved out. But only yesterday did I finish varnishing the floor.

Now I am trying to buy drop siding to do all the outside of the house with. That will make it warmer. I mean to put tar paper first, then drop siding, then paint it. That should discourage draughts. And I fear draughts. In fact I seem to notice them even when they are not there. I just can't stand draughts at all. They make my ear and my eye ache. Sometimes it is [the] right ear and eye: sometimes it is the left ones. And when they ache for a few hours, I begin to be sick. So I am all out to escape draughts.

The consulting room is just right. Eleven feet by eight and a half. It is painted cream. I did that. The waiting hall is just right too. It is four and a half feet by twelve feet. It is green, rather dark, halfway up: then cream on top. Ceilings in each case are painted cream. The waiting hall has one big comfortable armchair, like you get with a Chesterfield set. Also it has two wooden chairs and a wee table, which bears Eaton's Catalogue and the latest copy of 'Saturday Night', an illustrated news magazine. These, you have inferred, are to pass the time pleasantly for any who may have to wait. But I do not aim to keep people waiting, and I have not got very many patients. Still, even so, two lots are liable to arrive at the same time.

The bedroom is lined with Kraft's Sheeting, i.e. a thin cardboard, medium brown in colour. It looks all right. The ceiling is covered with it too. That should be windproof. It is pasted on: also tacked. The room is nine and a half feet by thirteen and a half feet. I have ordered a wardrobe for it. When it comes, I shall have everything, just right. In fact, it is such a nice little house now, that I am getting attached to it.

There are some things a little 'war-time' about it, particularly the varnish. I began by permanganating the old floor of the consulting room and hall. I did not so treat the new wood of the skirt [sic] boards, nor the bedroom floor.

I bought two tins of varnish, light oak and light mahogany and I mixed them. Maybe I did not ever mix them properly: or maybe the mahogany colour tended to settle down a bit. Anyway, the colour turned gradually to a redder tinge… I ran out of varnish. I bought a small tin of light oak, it was all there was, and a tin of walnut. So now the bedroom floor is walnut and light oak…and the skirt board mainly light mahogany. The stores cannot buy varnish now…I bought them out of all three kinds.

It is great fun fixing up a house.

The glory of my house is the chimney. It has a brick chimney, which looks lovely, sticking up through the roof. It is flush with the consulting room wall, but projects into my bedroom…I bought it nearly half a mile away and it was delivered here to me.

Sally clearly enjoyed her break in Canada but her heart was all the time in China and when the chance came to go back, she welcomed it eagerly. Her church and her three children needed her and her best work for her mission was still to come.

And so, in the spring of 1943, Sally set off once more. She went first to New Zealand and was accompanied by several Canadian missionaries.

Hilda Porter, of the Methodist Mission Society in London, wrote in April 1943 to William Wolfe of Skibbereen:

> … Sally [has] just received news that a passage was offered…to New Zealand.
>
> Speaking of the work she has left behind at Smeaton, she says that another doctor was available to take over and, had she not left at that moment, he would have had to do something else! "God's plans have a way of fitting in all round. I hope I shall arrive safely. But even if not I think it right to go now. Our times are in His hands and none of us would wish it otherwise. Many thanks for sanctioning my going". That is just Sally! And again reveals her wonderful spirit. I do pray that God will bring her safely to China which she loves and [to] the friends who are waiting for her.

Hilda Porter wrote again, in May 1943, to Sally's brother William in Canada. The Canadian letter is on one of those tiny airmail forms which were provided at the time, due to war regulations, and assures William that Sally has reached:

> ...some point on the journey and that the Secretary of the United Church of Canada believes it to be New Zealand. The boat on which they travelled from Canada was only going as far as New Zealand. I am not sure how much Sally told you before she left Canada but she has with her sufficient money to carry her through to India, unless there should be a very prolonged delay, in which case she has letters of introduction to the Conference of Missionary Societies both in New Zealand and Australia. Further, friends of the Methodist Church at both these points would gladly help in case she needs more. She has also letters of introduction to the Missionary Society in India, and there she will meet friends who will help her make arrangements to continue by air to China.

In April 1943, Sally writes to Fan from Auckland:

> O, it takes some getting used to, when you come here first. It is so hard to remember that the sun is north and your shadow south. But apart from that, and the differences that go with it, Auckland is like an English town. ...Mind you, I liked Canada well, when I was there. But this is more homelike....

And on 16th April, 1943, she writes to her brother, William:

> We have at last managed to get preferential rating for passages. So now we hope we may get to Australia by plane, sometime early in June. At first, we had only "ordinary" permits. And we were told it would be 5 or 6 months before our turn came. That was alarming, as of course we are using money all the time. We asked about ships. Of course, nobody will tell us anything. That was to be expected. But they did say that we have no chance at all for getting sea passage to Australia. This was a disappointment to us.

Today three of us went home from church with a lady and gentleman. We had dinner in their house. They were ever so nice to us. The man reports for a newspaper. He shewed us pictures of New Zealand, maps etc etc. He said he thinks there are 62 extinct volcanoes about Auckland, i.e. taking in a fairly wide area.... Fancy. I think this place must have boiled like a saucepan of toffee, long ago. And, of course, it could never have been like it is, only for that. It is lovely now.

I often thought that about our Kuling hill, too. It is a wonderful blessing to all central China. And it was certainly tossed up by an earthquake. Those great upheavals accomplish wonderful things....

... There is a museum here. It is better than I supposed, at my first visit. In fact, if I go a few more times, I shall probably have a high respect for it. Yesterday I studied specimens from Fiji and the Loyalty Islands. There are some interesting canoes in that room.

... I could turn into a Canadian in the course of time. It would take less time to turn me into a New Zealander. I don't wonder Uncle John liked this country. Is that rude to Canada? I don't mean it to be.

CHAPTER NINE

Back in China

Sally's destination in China was now Chungking, which was where the Mission had been relocated, having had to move west, ahead of the Japanese advance. In September 1943 Hilda Porter wrote to Fan:

> I am enclosing with this letter an extract from a letter which was sent by Mr J. J. Heady, describing something of what he saw when he went up to Chungking and Wanhsien...it gives some idea of where Sally will be....

The Reverend J. J. Heady writes:

> Chungking is quite an unusual and interesting place. The Yangtse flows between hills all along this stretch and the hills rise steeply on both banks at Chungking. On landing at the airfield, we had to go up about 240 steps before we came to the first street. There are steps all over the city in the same way.... It was good to see the place and quite good to see the old Yangtse once more, although of course it is not such a big river here 1,500 miles from the sea...I got on board the steamer for Wanhsien at 9 p.m. We left at dawn and arrived at Wanhsien just after dark. Rev K. K. Hsiao [who is] on the staff of Wesley College met us at the riverside.... In the morning Mr Hsiao took me on to Wesley

- about seven miles by rickshaw along a good motor road, and then eight miles by chair up the hills. It rained on the way up and we were wet in parts when we arrived.

The climate of the Yangtse valley is so different from that of Kunming. While at Chungking and Wanhsien, it was just like the old days at Hankow - hot and muggy. When I arrived back at Kunming it was so different - bracing and invigorating in comparison....

...Wesley has the use of a very large temple, overlooking the hills and valleys in a glorious sweep. They have built temporary classrooms and other necessary buildings - mud walls and wooden frames, but very well suited to their uses. They now have 515 boys and 116 girls in the school. They have begun taking girls since the Hanyang Girls' School had to close down in Hankow after Pearl Harbour. If only Miss Liu, the Hanyang School Headmistress could be here now, but...she died of typhoid soon after arriving in Chungking.

There are many of the old members of staff of Wesley here, and some more old Wesley boys who have recently joined up after taking their degrees. The total staff is 33, 28 are Christians. Most of the scholars are from the surrounding district. It is interesting that over 400 of the 631 scholars are the children of farmers. With the present high prices, farmers can afford to send their children to school and here is the school in their midst. That means that most of the scholars know little or nothing of Christianity. What an opportunity!

Sally wasn't so happy when she got there, arriving, presumably, in the same way - by steamer, rickshaw and chair. Here is her letter from the Wesley Middle School, dated 10th October, 1943 and sent to her sister Fan:

Here I am at last. It took me six and a half months to get here. And just now I am not finding things a bit satisfactory.

The school is about 15 miles out of the town: or anyway it takes 4-6 hours to get to it. It is up in the hills. All around here, there is nothing but hills.

There are about 600 students in the school: packed in this way :- they lie side by side along each side of the dormitories: not sideways, like on board ship: heads all to wall, feet to passage. Downstairs there are three tiers of them: upstairs two tiers. It is terribly crowded. We hope to have a few new dormitories soon, and to ease it a bit.

Our folks got the lend of a Buddhist Temple, for the school. Then they ran up mud buildings and are still doing so. At present I live a mile away from the school. It is not satisfactory. The path is steep and narrow: in many places it is a flight of irregular stone steps. I come down it very cautiously in wet weather: i.e. if I have to. I stay at home most wet days. Because there is no way of avoiding getting my feet and legs all wet: and I go sick so easily now.

But soon they will have a new block up and I am to live in it. I fear it will be a month or more yet. I don't like being here at all. I am too useless. It will be much better when I can live on the spot.

The scenery is magnificent: and the people are friendly; but all of them are very busy. Country people always are, unless in winter.

Johan is with me. He was 8 months in hospital in Chungking. I owe a whopping bill for that. He has a nasty tubercular sinus all along one side of his rectum. It is very nasty. But he sleeps a lot and eats well. He sleeps about 11 hours at night: and about 2 or 3 by day. He is very good about it. I have him here, just doing nothing. Sometimes we read a bit of English (his English is fairly good). He borrowed *Robinson Crusoe* but it is really a bit difficult for him. However, I have nothing better.

This house is a C.I.M. summer bungalow. And at present we have a little old baby-organ in it. That won't be here very long though. But while it is he plays it a bit. I taught him a few hymns etc five years ago. He learned quickly and well. He still can play several of them, after all that time. Soon he will know them all again. ... He has considerable skill in vamping, too. His ear is good. He can sing any of the four parts of a number of hymns.

Today, he played 'Jesus, pilot me' quite nicely. I asked him if he had learned it by himself. For I had not taught it to him. He said he had not learned it at all, but he 'perceived' that the harmonies went rather like that. I was ever so pleased…if he were taught, he could be a musician. He sings either tenor or base: probably should be tenor. But in many hymns he prefers bass.

Prices here are outrageous: much higher than in Canada. But that is largely because people are not confident about the value of paper money.

I saw Suteh in Chungking. In fact, I was there the day she got her cap. It is usual to take new nurses on probation for 3-6 months and after that those who want to stay on wear caps. So now Suteh is an accepted pupil nurse of the Canadian Mission Hospital. She has done well so far and is happy. I have not seen Futeh. But if an opportunity offers, I want her to come here. She is in Hunan.

The climate here is wetter than where we used to be: and it gets terribly cold when it comes wet: in fact, it is unbelievably cold. But they say the winters are not very cold: not as cold as in Hankow. I hope that is so. For I have been finding it impossible to keep warm here in September and October! And then the sun comes out and it is summer again.

So now you know our circumstances. Today I led a little service: only three neighbours and ourselves. We will see later: at present, I don't seem able to do much. The neighbours don't come to the school service at all: they feel inferior. And so far I have not got anywhere. We are a fortnight behind world news.

Hilda Porter wrote to Fan and William Wolfe on 13th December, 1943:

I am very grateful indeed for your having shared with me this most interesting letter from Sally.

I am glad to note that, while she is housed in the C.I.M. mission about a mile from the school, she is not venturing down to the school in bad weather. I feel sure that she will take care and, judging by the letters from Mr Richardson, I expect the building on the school compound to which she is going, will be ready within a few weeks. I hope that she will be as comfortable as it is possible for evacuated folk to be there.

Awfully sorry to hear that Johan still has a nasty tubercular sinus, but it is good to know that he is eating and sleeping well and putting on weight. Very sorry indeed to hear about the terrible expense that Sally has been put to while Johan has been in hospital. I'll see if I can do something to help towards this, for I am sure that Sally, herself, ought not to meet all that extra cost.

At the beginning of this year I did put into Sally's Personal Account in this House, monies that she had not drawn. Indeed, she said she did not need them, but I felt the time would come when she might need the money. The total amounts paid into her account here were £125.0.0. and it looks as if the whole of that has been completely swallowed up and more. But then, if everything is a hundred times what it used to be, £100.0.0. is a mere nothing.

There now follows a gap in information - no-one seems to have kept any letters for the years 1943 to 1947. Maybe there weren't many. The war ended in 1945 and Soviet troops drove the Japanese out of Manchuria. However, contrary to the Communists' expectations, the Soviets backed Chiang Kai-shek and the Kuomintang as the legitimate government of China. Once more, civil war between the Kuomintang and the Communists broke out. The Communists concentrated first on Manchuria and then moved south.

The following letter from Sally was found in her sister Fan's diary. Fan often sent letters on to the family in Canada, copying the original first. In this case, she has simply made her own summary of the contents. Sally's letter was sent from Chungsiang. This town is in Hupeh Province, in the middle of Eastern China, well away from Manchuria, yet it clearly had its disturbances. Later it was to become a frontline in the civil war.

She wrote from the Methodist General Hospital on 13th November, 1947.

U.N.R.R.A. (United Nations Relief and Rehabilitation Administration) have been distributing left-over Allied Army Medical Supplies to Chinese hospitals. Mission hospitals got a nice lot of very good things; Government hospitals got even more.

The stuff was delivered free, but required the hospital concerned to put a responsible person on the truck, to take charge of the things. There was a broken bridge near a hot spring. Sallie [sic] was the responsible person in charge for her hospital. She had often passed the hot spring before but never had a chance to have a good look at it. She was glad to examine it now.

Sally and her colleagues were fortunate that the goods, sent to them by U.N.R.R.A. (post-war American relief), were useful, for some of what was handed out to the civilian population by the organisation was not always so appropriate. Powdered milk no doubt had its place but the tins of cheese that they also sent were of little use to the Chinese people, who did not and probably could not eat such things, finding them disgusting and indigestible. Butter was also sent. The missionaries called it 'rubber butter', because of its consistency - it bounced when you touched it and was cheese coloured but tasted good. Clothing was included in the handouts, some of it in the form of bales of cloth. Some administrators had the good sense to get the rolls of cloth cut into dress lengths before releasing them. They did this in an attempt to limit the abuse that inevitably happened, which was that most of the aid ended up on the black market. Most inappropriate of all were the high-heeled shoes included in some consignments.

Fan's notes on Sally's letter continue:

> She (Sallie) has part of a house. Jack Chamberlayne occupies the rest of the house.
>
> Wusueh, one of their mission stations, had a raid recently. Rev Livesley, senior, and Rev Gilliland, very junior, on the staff there. Livesley was away at an out-station. Gilliland is Irish. They did not bother him beyond searching the house, but the Chinese minister, an old man, got two bullets in his leg. The regular troops turned up a day or two later and sent the raiders away again. This sort of thing kept happening 12 to 20 years ago.
>
> Suteh had a nasty accident. She got a finger infected when doing midwifery. It would not heal, so they tested for syphilis and got a positive result. They gave penicillin and other things, and she is apparently all right. "But that sort of thing is just a terror to see the last of." Poor girl!

Futeh writes happily from Hanyang. Sallie has had a letter recently from Johan which said: "I am blither than last year."

(He was fairly 'blithe' last year too!)

She wishes he and Futeh were stronger. Suteh was always fine until this accident.

Evangelism is easier there than [in] Hankow, which is all right, too.

They need a matron of experience; she thinks they will soon have the former matron, Lydia Lee, back. Mrs Rowley used sometimes to appeal to Dr Cundall against her. He was apt to say "Ah, well, I must go down and put the lid on Lydia", but she is a good sort and teaches well, also economic and does not waste things.

Suteh has married Wu Ying Seng in May 1948. A letter dated 11th September, 1948 and copied ('more or less') into Fan's diary gives interesting information about her:

I arrived back here a week ago. Things have changed a lot since I left. But it is not a time of free discussion of many matters. The city has been largely pulled down and all the elaborate fortifications that were built outside the suburbs are demolished. Right here we have peace. But the countryside is lawless. There is little business going on. We have no post office. You would think the town looks strange indeed.

Li Si Fu, my servant, and I made the trip from Hankow in 10 days. (If we would have peace and buses running again, it takes about 8 hours). Seven days by water, the last three overland.

Suteh was still working in the Union Hospital, but she meant to go to her home probably next month. She thinks she may have a babe in March. She was not looking very well. The rooms are very hot in summer. But all the great heat is past now.

Futeh is living with her people-in-law. They wish it. And she is pleased that they do. She is a gay little soul. Her man is studying at Nanking. The family live just outside Wuchang, across the river from Hankow.

Suteh and Wu Ying Seng, on their wedding day, 16th May, 1948.
With Martin and Barbara Russell.

Johan is not settled. He had another operation this summer and was still in hospital when I came away. I arranged that he should share a room with a teacher in our day school, as soon as he left hospital. He is probably doing that now. I hope he may get a light teaching job. It is very bad for him to be idle. But nothing was settled when I left.

He made his affairs hard to handle when he got betrothed to a Mohammedan. She is Christian now. But her family take no notice of him. He wants to learn drawing. But this term he has to stay right by the hospital. If he could make the journey here, I could look after his wound myself. But with the whole region seething with unrest, that is impossible. I can only leave him in Hankow. Hwei Dyen, his girl, is getting along all right with her training as a nurse.

Coming back here I toppled off a donkey…I was afraid I was hurt, but I wasn't. I am moving fairly freely again after 9 days.

The hospital has got into careless ways. Some of the pupil nurses won't do as they are told and answer back cheekily if the seniors say anything to them…. Our Miss Li Yu Lan, who would be a great standby if well, has very poor health the last few years. She won't let anyone examine her. So we do not really know what ails her. But she is beginning to look as if it may be a cancer. She has had it, whatever it is, for three years, so treatment of cancer now is impossible even if it were diagnosed. I all the time think what a pity it is she can't be well. But God knows best.

However difficult things may be, it is good to be here. If our Christian church can stand quietly and steadily at this time, it will be a witness not easily gainsaid. It is very important to keep the churches together. It is the witness of the whole group that counts, not so much what anyone may say or do. But in so far as I can at all shepherd a few folks these times, I am very glad to be here. And I know well they are glad to have me. We do help things to cohere.

I came back at my own responsibility. The chairman and the consul do not take responsibility for that move. They cannot. Our church folks decided that each of us is free to decide for himself, under the guidance of God, what he ought to do. So here I am, with the knowledge and approval of the chairman but without any instructions from him and solely on my own responsibility.

So, should anything untoward happen, do not even think or say that the Mission should not have sent me here. They did not, not this time. I came. And I know God willed it. He brought us in perfect peace through much disturbed country. And all the way my heart was at perfect peace: or would have been, even if we had failed to get here.

I enjoy life. I am all on for living. But should I die, that would not be matter for much regret. The last years of old age, like Aunt Sarah's or Aunt Rachel's, do not seem to offer much that can be coveted. But I shall not do anything foolhardy. I love the world and the things that are in the world. But you will easily see that we cannot withdraw in the face of atheism. We must stand and we should as far as possible stand in our original grouping. I shall send this letter by hand to Hankow. And once in a way I hope I may get letters from Hankow. Yet we are probably more cut off now than we were during the Japanese occupation. Address letters "Hankow". If you put "Chung Siang" the post office will return them to you.

The hospital is full. The day school has over 300 pupils. The women's school has over 10. They are embarrassed by the presence of soldiers. Except for drawing water and washing things around our well, they scarcely come on to this compound, which is across the road from the women's school…. Letters coming and going here are sure to be very slow. So don't be surprised if mine become very infrequent.

But another letter reached Fan from Chungsiang, dated 28th November, 1948:

…I had a happy letter from Suteh two days ago. She is still working in hospital, says she is fat and well and puts in her off-duty time making little garments: has knitted a cap and a pair of stockings and made various tiny garments. It is a nice happy letter. She hopes for a babe in early March, if it is not late February.

We have had five months of peace here and our work was not hindered in any way, except for the inconvenience of not having any postal communication. Last Tuesday we were recaptured by the national army, quite a big section of it. They lopped a few shells here and there, to announce their advent. One killed a child on our compound and slightly hurt 6 folks. As there was no return fire, they soon discovered that their coming was unresisted. We asked them why they fired on us. They replied that it was a mistake: they thought we had a big communist army holding the city. Well, we hadn't.

There were a few soldiers about, almost up to the time the national army came in. But they made no attempt at all to hold the city: nor any preparation for such an attempt. We knew all along that they would not try to hold the city. Well, they are gone: and they were a wee bit too slow in going.

We got an enormous army instead of them. All money became useless. Trade is abolished.

Now we hear that this enormous army is a very good one (it looks it), too good to waste its sweetness where there are only a few guerrillas. So they say they are leaving us again.

It is all burdensome to the people. You don't half know the value of peace: nor the burden a big army is. But once they are here, folks would like them to leave a garrison. Changing sides is always fraught with danger. And now, as always, the question is "What next?" But "hitherto the Lord helped us".

I am well. I contemplate a visit to Hankow, if it seems reasonably safe. The weather is cold. The hospital is not so busy these days, because folks have to stay at home owing to having soldiers billeted on them. We were very busy until Tuesday and doubtless will be again quite soon. Never a dull moment.

Sally wrote again to Fan from Chungsiang on 2nd October, 1949:

I had better start by wishing you a happy Christmas. For I write so few letters now, another may be late. Things are pretty much as they were when I last wrote. We see all the patients that come, and admit about 60-70 or more, if they want to come in. We have been very busy this past month.

Our matron is leaving us, at very short notice. It is really my fault. She asked for a rise of salary and thought the rise I offered her was too small. I am sorry she left like that. But I have called on her since and I think we may count as friends in spite of her leaving. Her departure lands us in difficulty with the teaching. Hilda [Hilda Shepherd, a mission nurse] and the other nurses will have to do a lot, until we can get another matron. I was doing 5 hours a week, anyway. Now I shall do 6. That is all I can do to help over the difficult time. I have the hospital accounts, and the oversight of everything in a general way.

I am well. So is Hilda. Neither of us is very fat. I say I am fatter than she is. She says she is fatter than I am.

We are allowed to assemble for public worship. There is no direct hindrance at all to our work: only a definite anti-Christian atmosphere. Of course, you know communists are atheists. But lots of them are quite nice folks.

I have a nice little photo of Suteh's baby, when she was four months old. Futeh invited her out to have it taken, and, of course, paid for it. It was rather a nice thing for Futeh to do, wasn't it? The baby is a paragon, placid and friendly and ready to smile at anyone. She answers when spoken to. She is called 'Lee Lee,' after me. They tried 'Sa Lee' and found it awkward. So they dropped the 'Sa' and doubled the 'Lee.' It is usual to duplicate syllables in baby talk. 'Lee' means 'white jasmine flower'. It is a nice name.

Johan was fatter than I have seen him for years. i.e. when I saw him last July. I made a trip to Hankow in July and saw them all. It was a hasty trip, with very little time in Hankow. But I had to buy medicines. Now international relations seem to be worsening. For when Hilda asked for a permit to go to Hankow to fetch her winter clothes, it was refused. Or at least it was not refused: only it was not granted: the request was just dropped....

… We have a post-office now. But it is not a bit easy to write letters. Everyone seems to feel the same about it.

Last Saturday this place was searched at dawn. Everyone was courteous. They took one graduate nurse and one pupil (a boy). But later in the day we were allowed to bail them out. It did them no harm, only they missed their breakfast and lunch. They were offered food, all right.

A month or so ago there was talk of getting a Dr Chang to come here as superintendent. I have heard nothing about him since then. I expect he wanted too high a salary. But I don't know. The whole countryside is poor. Some places are still flooded. The river kept high a month later than it usually does. Our own immediate neighbourhood was not flooded, although there was great uneasiness about it for a long time. Now the river is a little lower. It should be safe now.

… Don't worry about me, even if you don't hear from me. The authorities are quite courteous to me. Don't forget me in your prayers. The need of prayer for the coming of God's Kingdom on earth was never greater.

'Don't worry about me' she says. Of course, they did and with justification. If my hunches are right, this is probably the period when she was hiding in a pigsty from searching soldiers and operating for such long, back-breaking hours that she had to get two nurses to straighten her up every now and again so that she could keep going. (See chapter 5).

Writing to Fan from Hankow on 5th March, 1950, Sally claims to be in better health and so is returning to Chungsiang:

Hilda Shepherd would have to leave if I left, at least that is the attitude of our mission. As to whether she would be permitted to leave, we have no certain knowledge. Foreigners are not allowed to move about much. But I think that if we wished to leave finally, we would get passes.

It is very hard to tell you much about Communism.

There is a lot that is good in it: and a lot that is contradictory: and the amount of time wasted about everything is just ruinous.

You can't do the simplest thing without calling a committee and spending hours talking about it. We would rather get ahead and do it. But that is not permissable. Apart from this, and their well-known atheism, they do quite well. They have certainly captured the loyalty of the teen and twenty age folks....

... Dr Hsien is now medical superintendent. I shall not have any great responsibility and "may be recalled at any time," so say the Medical Committee who station us. This is put in to try to get Dr Hsien not to try to thrust responsibility on to me. I hope I can work at least another six months.

The letter goes on to give us the first clue that Johan has indeed married his Muslim girlfriend, Hwei Dyen.

Suteh's Lee Lee can walk, though not quite a year old. Hwei Dyen's babe is expected about 20th April. Suteh and her folks are all well: so is Futeh. Hwei Dyen is well, too: but Johan is not looking very well.

I rather think I may be home by Christmas: but I don't know at all. If things were normal, with free travel for new-comers, I should leave at once.

"As thy days, so shall thy strength be."

However, she is still in China on 7th January, 1951 when she writes to her sister Kitty in Canada:

...I am fairly well: but I am never quite as well in cold weather as at other times. I have sent in a statement that I wish to leave Chungsiang on 6th March, to leave China by 31st March. But the police told me not to apply for an exit permit just now. So this statement is only, so to speak, a preliminary notice. Whether or not I shall get a permit about that time remains to be seen. For the convenience of the hospital I cannot well leave earlier.

Hilda means to ask for a permit to leave with me. At first, she thought of staying on for a year or so in Hankow. But money is becoming difficult and the mission house wish most of us to leave. They suggested our trying to leave earlier. But, as I have said, the convenience of the hospital requires us to stay till the end of February: and the police told me twice not to raise the question of exit permits now. So I cannot well approach them on the matter at present.

We are in the process of being registered as aliens: which process called for 10 photographs of each of us! We had previously within a month supplied the police with 4 photographs of each of us. So I have ordered another dozen! The police have been very nice to us about this registration, as they have been about other things.

They questioned me for 2 hours in the forenoon, and Hilda for 2 hours in the afternoon: asked all about our past, present and future: then about our relations and friends, what you all do, where you live etc. I don't think there is very much left for them to ask.

Our new Dr Hu seems to be settling in happily. We all like him. And he is more sensible than our last doctor. One small matter:- Dr Lin began by quarrelling with our dog: and our dog insisted on keeping up the matter. Dr Hu began by making friends with that dog, and the dog loves him, and walks with him, wagging his tail and expressing his pleasure at being in his company. That is only one minor matter. But Dr Hu is nice. Everyone likes him.

Just now we are holding examinations: nine pupil nurses up for their finals. So the wards are short-handed. Some of these nurses are worth keeping. I hope our matron won't let them all go, like she did our last class. Of them she only kept one, a relative of her own, and a really troublesome girl. But perhaps the matron can guide her a bit.

The land around here is being partitioned out into small lots. While this is being done, all public meetings are forbidden. So this is the 3rd Sunday we have had no public worship. All the church members are sad about it. But it is only for the duration of the land division. We hope to resume services after that.

Presumably, all the Christian denominations were suffering the same restrictions. A relative recalls Sally saying that the Roman Catholic Mission was just behind the Methodist compound and that they were very helpful to the Methodists but she does not recall just how.

On the subject of the compound, one of Sally's nieces remembers being told the following anecdote by Sally. It must have occurred about this time, when the Communist clampdown on them was getting tougher:

> It was one evening shortly before she left China, when the Communists were in control of the whole area. It had been a busy day and Sally went out to walk in the cool of the garden. The compound had a wall running round it and a soldier was stationed outside. Of course, he could only hear her so he called to ask her who she was and what she was doing. She identified herself. He said she ought not to be out and to go back. Sally said:
>
> "I put a smile into my voice and said that, after all, this was my garden and I had a perfect right to walk in it. And he put a smile into his voice and said nothing."

Some might think the turn of phrase unlikely but those of us who knew Sally know better: it precisely illustrates her unusual way of saying things, her sense of humour and her understanding of mankind.

Sally, as she revealed in her letter to her sister Kitty, wanted to leave China by the end of March but obstacles were put in her way by the authorities. Protestant missionaries were rarely deported, I am told. Instead, most opted to go, like Sally, because life had become just too difficult and even more because their presence as foreigners damaged the Chinese church in the eyes of the Communists. When it became clear that more harm than good was being done, it was time to leave. An entry in Fan's diary for 20th April, 1951, reports: 'Letter from Sally, saying she has applied for an exit permit.'

Application for an exit permit would only have been the beginning. When the Reverend Desmond Gilliland and his family did the same, they had first to place an advertisement in the newspapers. Then they were told they had to obtain a guarantee from a Chinese resident, confirming their good behaviour during the whole of their stay in China.

No-one in the local church would have dared to provide such a thing.

The Gillilands, however, found a very brave man who agreed to do it for them - a male nurse in the hospital who was not even a Christian. When Desmond went to him and asked him if he would do it, he immediately said yes. The man's wife was very anxious about it and pulled at his coat, trying to stop him, but he paid no attention to her. Desmond has sometimes worried since that this brave action on the nurse's part might have caused him trouble later.

Next, the departing missionaries had to furnish lists of their possessions in triplicate and finally submit to a detailed interview by a government official. The Gillilands' first application was rejected and they had to subject themselves to a second rigorous interview before being allowed to leave.

Desmond Gilliland tells this lovely story about his father-in-law's departure from China. He was Dr Cundall, who was a contemporary of Sally's and whose work as a medical missionary in China is legendary:

> … In Hankow the examination of foreigners about to leave was conducted by a man we called the Sphinx, because he was completely aloof, inscrutable, unsmiling, disdainful, exacting the last detail of compliance with the regulations….
>
> My father-in-law… was asked if he had infringed Chinese law during his time in China. Unable to resist a quip, even in those circumstances, Dr Cundall asked if it included the law of the Ch'ing dynasty, the Sun Yat Sen Republic, the Regnum of Yuan Shih K'ai, the Kuomintang, or the Peoples Republic, as he had been there for all of them. The Sphinx did not move a muscle and completed the interrogation with his usual aloofness.
>
> When the inspection was finished a strange thing happened. The dreaded Sphinx came round to the other side of the barrier and said - in English - "On that side of the barrier I am a Chinese official, performing my duty. On this side I speak for myself. I wish to thank you for all your service to our Chinese people." He even smiled. It was a good epitaph to one man's missionary career.

All of which could equally well have happened to Sally. We do know that the Communists thought highly of her, for a nephew of hers recalls being told of how she once infringed some rule or other which the Communists had imposed. The punishment for doing this was imprisonment but the local authorities considered her to be too venerable to be arrested and so they arrested Hilda Shepherd instead!

She was certainly revered by the Chinese who worked with her in the hospital and before she left they presented her with two beautiful scrolls which prove it. They are about six feet in length and a foot wide and are made of tough, deep red paper and have gold Chinese script written on them, in two vertical lines, one line being much smaller than the other. One scroll when translated reads:

'She healed the entire globe and jewels are made more precious by her virtue.'

And the other reads:

'Her name is known throughout China and foreign countries and her virtue enriches gold.'

It seems she and Hilda Shepherd left China together. A cousin remembers being told that the two women were among the last to get out of China and that they had to make a hazardous journey down river by boat, being fired on all the way. The river was presumably the Yangtse and if that is the route they took, they would have eventually reached Hankow and then presumably on to Shanghai. The Gillilands, however, went south by rail, to Hong Kong.

I remember Sally telling me about the situation she left behind. How the Communists had clamped down on the country, imposing rigid barriers on each region, so that a person who found himself resident in one area could not under any circumstances travel to another.

The situation affected Futeh particularly badly. She was living with her future in-laws in Wuchang, outside Hankow (Hupeh district) and her fiancé was at Nanking University, (Chiangsu district). With Sally's departure, Futeh had no official home. There must have been great dangers inherent in the situation, for in the end her fiancé's parents decided to adopt her as their daughter. The solution, though, was a tragic one, for it meant she then became her fiancé's sister and so could never marry him.

Suteh, of course, was married already. As for Johan, one story has it that

Sally's niece Marjorie Christmas holds up the gold and red scroll that proclaims: 'Her name is known throughout China and foreign countries and her virtue enriches gold.'

he was conscripted into the army. We know, of course, that he was married and presumably Hwei Dyen had been safely delivered of her child. Sally must have worried a great deal about him on account of everything - his bad health, his unsettled disposition and his enforced life in the army, if that is indeed what happened to him.

One wonders how they all fared. China went through some very turbulent times as the Communists established their regime. Hopefully, her children and their families survived and their Christian upbringing brought them comfort and strength. Sally, as I said at the start of this story and as far as we know, never heard another word about or from her children, for all communication with the West, including letter writing, was stopped. Given the sort of things that we now know did happen to others, perhaps it was as well that she remained in ignorance.

On the other hand, I don't suppose she would have let it prey on her mind too much, for she would have put her trust in God and I, along with others, never remember her seeming particularly worried about anything.

We now know that two of China's upheavals were especially damaging. They were the Great Leap Forward of the late 1950's and the Cultural Revolution of 1966.

The Great Leap Forward began in 1957 and was an economic movement for which Mao Tse-tung was responsible. Everything and everyone was sacrificed to meet its ends, those ends being a crazy attempt to match and then outstrip the industrial production of the West, in as short a time as possible.

Steel production was one of the main areas chosen for this effort. People devoted their waking hours to scrabbling about for scraps of metal and bits of wood to feed the hungry steel furnaces. They threw in their cooking utensils and cut down their woods and forests, neglecting their fields and crops in the process. All, of course, to little purpose for there was no way such an approach could achieve what was intended. The only result was that other areas of life, such as agriculture, were neglected and the steel produced in this makeshift way was of too inferior a quality to be useful, anyway.

Farms were put together into communes and the farm workers were told to make massive improvements in their food production. At the same time, the State took over the distribution of this food and set the limits on how much each commune could keep for itself. Peasants, whose way of life had always involved an arduous but individual struggle to feed themselves and their families, now found that responsibility taken from them.

Meanwhile, huge false production totals were recorded to satisfy the officials. The result was that much of the actual harvest was diverted to the towns while the farm workers used up what was left, feeling safe in the knowledge that the State would now provide for their needs and that China was awash with produce. Since most of the government propaganda was false, a terrible famine set in between 1959-61, during which over 30 million Chinese died.

In 1966 Mao inaugurated The Cultural Revolution, where he stirred up the young and called on them to smash anything that was perceived as being old and decadent in the country. His stated aim was to 'purify' the Communist state but in reality he was trying to eliminate anyone who might try to challenge his position. The movement gave the young a free rein and many responded with enthusiasm.

Even some of those who had always considered themselves good, loyal Communists now found themselves in trouble and anyone with a 'suspect' background was particularly at risk. A missionary upbringing would undoubtedly have been a handicap during these years. Teachers were another group which suffered badly. Many of their pupils joined the Red Guards and turned against their instructors as easy targets - beating them up, torturing them, even killing them. If Johan did become a teacher, as Sally at one time clearly hoped he would, he could hardly have escaped this sort of treatment. However, all of this is, of course, speculation.

Religion in China is not so frowned on today and many of the old missionary hospitals are now flourishing as state hospitals and medical care has greatly increased, all built on the sure foundations of the dedication and sacrifice of those early pioneers. So the medical missionaries have clearly left a lasting legacy.

CHAPTER TEN

Return

Fan's diary for 7th May, 1951, records: 'Letter from Sally, saying she is in Hong Kong.'

I recall her talking of the passage from China to Hong Kong. How she had had to travel third class (she always did so, anyway, but on previous occasions had been allowed second class privileges). The ship was appallingly overcrowded and the conditions on board were terrible. She maintained her fastidious cleanliness by waking early to listen out for the cleaners and using the washroom facilities directly after they had finished with them.

On 8th July, 1951 Sally again wrote to Fan from *S.S. Carthage*, the ship which was bringing her home:

> I shall post this on board. But when you get it you will know I have reached London.
>
> As you know, I am concerned about my eyes. Dr Ralph Bolton has arranged consultation for me as soon as I arrive. I am glad of this. I have, of course, committed my eyes, as the rest of me, to God. However it turns out it will be alright. I am not worried. But I want to do the best for a pair of eyes that have served me well and long.
>
> As soon as I know how things are I shall write to you. Meantime I expect to be in London for ten days or so. That brings us to time of Betty's coming. Please arrange to meet her without me.

It will be nicer for all of you…

… I have   1 Cabin trunk

              1 Wooden trunk

              1 Cedar wood case. (If it is not bashed to bits).
There are actually two, one inside the other.

I shall ask Cook's representative what to do with them. He may suggest sending them on to you, in which case they would arrive about the 17th to 20th…

…I go as a guest to Dr Bolton, 2 days, 2 days to Hilda Porter and cannot take all my stuff to either place; nor is there need to pay the double duty.

It will be nice to see you again. I tell you again, I am old like Grandma used to be, not like Mammy was when you knew her.

A week later, on 14th July, she wrote again to Fan:

> … It is not yet decided just exactly what is wrong with my eyes, nor whether they require active treatment or not. Meantime, my sight is better and I have no pain at all. I never had much, but I used to keep getting some all the time, on and off. I had hoped for more agreement among my advisers!
>
> You have rooms at Courtown Harbour. I do not even know where it is. Near Dublin? I could come there about 31st July if that is best…

And Fan's diary tells us that on 31st July she did arrive and Fan was 'greatly relieved to see her so strong and sight so good, also she dressed in colours'.

Sally's arrival in Ireland more or less coincided with the return of my family on an extended 'Home Leave' from Kenya. My mother, Betty, rented a house in Dublin for a year and Fan and Sally joined us. I was nine at the time, my sister, Felicity, six and my brother Robert four.

First impressions can be deceptive. I do not remember Sally as being very strong. She stayed with us most of that year and I remember my mother saying later that she feared Sally might have a breakdown, so great was the stress she seemed to be suffering. However, Sally was too strong for that to happen. One thing helped her greatly during that time and that was the special relationship she formed with Robert. Sally loved small children, as her letters so clearly reveal. Robert was train-mad at that age and every day he and Sally went down the road to Milltown station to watch trains. The shared activity and interest must have been a balm to her battered spirits.

At the end of the year, my family went back to Kenya and not long afterwards Sally went out to join her brothers and sister and their families in Canada.

She stayed in Canada till 1957, occasionally working but mostly occupying herself with her relations and their lives. We know that she relieved a Dr Savage at Cold Lake Hospital for at least one summer. Cold Lake was then just a fishing village, about fifty miles from Elk Point and is on the Alberta-Saskatchewan border. Her brother Tom was still living at Elk Point but her brother William and his wife had moved to Victoria, where they ran a nursing home, Hollandia House. Sally sometimes helped in the running of this nursing home and occasionally took over completely so that her relatives could go on holiday.

However, the amount she could do was severely limited, for in 1953 she slipped and fell in her brother Tom's kitchen at Elk Point. The accident resulted in a broken hip which was so badly set that she could only walk thereafter with the aid of a wooden crutch, being unable to put her full weight on her damaged leg.

It was a disability that probably need not have happened. A young, inexperienced surgeon in the local hospital was quite sure he could set her hip and persuaded her to let him try. He should have sent her off to a larger hospital, far away as that no doubt was, for his confidence in himself was misplaced. Sally's reaction to the mistake was quite typical - I am told she never once uttered a word of blame or criticism towards him nor did I ever hear her complain of any pain, discomfort or even inconvenience.

Needless to say, she didn't let her disability stand in her way. Years later she stayed with my mother in our home in Ireland. There was a particularly nice view to be had at the end of a long, uphill woodland path but to see it one had to climb over a wall into a neighbour's field. The walk up was a good half mile and the wall at the end of it was about three foot high and made of large, loose boulders. Without telling anyone, Sally set off to see the view. I accidentally came upon her up there, where the wind blew fresh and cold, sitting on a grassy bank at the edge of the field and looking out at the sea. She looked at me and I looked at her but neither of us spoke: though I was nearly grown up I almost thought I was hallucinating and that in that wild Irish hilly countryside some leprechaun or something had taken her form. It was a very weird sensation. I sensed that she didn't want to be interrupted and that she was enjoying her achievement in getting there.

When we asked her afterwards how she managed the wall, she said she simply threw her crutch over first, then hauled herself up on to the wall and rolled off it. A procedure which she had to do, of course, twice, in order to get back. How she avoided breaking further bones, I do not know.

Sally left Canada and came back to live in Cork in 1957. In a way, it was a surprising move. Letters written to her niece, Linda, during 1957, when Sally was still in Canada and Linda was away from home, have a ring of happiness to them and show her to have been deeply interested in her nephews and nieces and their doings. She even went on a radio quiz show with her niece Mona and Mona's fiancé and clearly thoroughly enjoyed the new experience, even though they did not win.

Then, in spite of all this, she decided to leave. Possibly her incapacitated state had something to do with her decision, in that the cold Canadian winters probably didn't suit her. The reason she gave us when we asked her, however, was that she wanted to die in Ireland.

Sally joined her sister Fan who was living in a flat in Cork city. The flat was in a medium-sized semi-detached house called Cedargrove on the Western Road and Sally got a separate flat in the same house. Sally and Fan had never been particularly close and Fan's vagueness, fey imagination and muddle clearly irritated Sally slightly. Willie had died and Fan was getting used to her own independence and was enjoying it. She loved going to the cinema and taking her lunches out in city restaurants. These were interests which Sally did not share but nevertheless they managed to get along.

They both got enjoyment out of their landlady, Mrs Mundt, who lived with her husband in another apartment in the same house. Fan and she had become good friends. Mrs Mundt was a most unusual woman. She had been left the house by former employers whose handicapped child she had looked after. Being a builder's daughter, she had personally carried out most of the amazing renovations on the property she owned. I recall a strange little kitchenette that opened (unfolding, as it were) out of a cupboard on the upstairs landing and Fan's bathroom door which had a bolt on the outside but none on the inside.

The flats were not exactly compact - Fan's bedroom was upstairs, her sitting room downstairs, at the front of the house, and her kitchen and bathroom in an extension thrown out into the garden. Sally's flat was in what was called 'the annexe' and was, I am sure, equally unconventional. It does not sound as if it was the most comfortable place to live in, either. In a letter to a niece in Canada, dated 23rd October, 1958, Sally said that she had 'gone stiff' and had trouble getting on and off the bus. So 'I sit in front of the radiator, or lie in bed with a hot water bottle, and generally take care of myself.'

In this letter she also mentions that they had a sermon from Professor Ernest Walton of Trinity College, Dublin. He was one of the two men who split the atom seven years previously and he got the Nobel prize for it. The sermon was on 'Our Faith in the Atomic Age' and she enjoyed both it and the man, whose sister -in-law she knew particularly well.

The letter ends with a typical family anecdote:

> Seven years ago, the school that he [Ernest Walton] formerly attended [Methodist College, Belfast] gave a holiday in honour of that Nobel prize. A junior cousin of ours came home early and when his mother asked him what the half holiday was for, he said "O, I don't know. Some fellow broke something."

'Fame', Sally comments, 'has its limits.'

Both Mr and Mrs Mundt unexpectedly died in the autumn of 1962 and Fan and Sally had to find alternative accommodation. By then my own family had come back from Kenya and were living in West Cork and Fan went back to Skibbereen to be near us. Sally went to live with a cousin, Marie Kingston, in her bungalow Sicaun, near Carrigaline. Sally was much more comfortable there than she had been in the flat at Mrs Mundt's and Marie showered her with attention and care. It was a God-given arrangement, each offering the other something she needed. They lived together happily until Marie became ill and then they both moved into St Luke's Home on Military Hill in Cork.

There Sally suffered another fall and broke her hip again. This time she was left bedridden. The fall was due to her usual independence - she wanted to get something off the top of a wardrobe and instead of asking someone to do it for her, climbed up on a chair and accidentally pulled the wardrobe over so that it fell on her. When her friend and minister, the late Reverend George Good, next visited her, he expressed concern at her injuries and spoke of the shock she must have had when it happened. She just smiled at him and replied;

"Aye, I did get a bit of a fright."

He recalled being sent for on one occasion during these last years, when it was thought Sally was dying. She had been taken to the Victoria Hospital but within a day had made a miraculous recovery and she expressed relief at this, not because she was afraid of dying but because her death would have been an inconvenience to the family, a member of whom was getting married in the following week.

Not only was she now bedridden but she had also more or less lost her sight through glaucoma. None of this seemed to get her down. For years she had resorted to typing letters and continued to do so in St Luke's.

Here is a letter I received in 1969 as I was about to get married. I include it merely to illustrate her enormous determination not to let a misfortune such as bad sight get in her way. The missing letters were due to the fact that the ribbon on the typewriter was so worn.

Sally, about 1958.

129

                                   St Lukes Home
                    Military Hill
                    C

                        ork
                        .9 pl 969
                                        or there bouts

Dear Jane

    any thanks for our letter. It was good of you to write. I m very
happy about your engagement. I am all in f vour of young folks
pairing themselves off, nd m rrying. It is the right thing for
most of them. I hope yours will be a happ union, and one that
lasts long…

    …You r grandma wrote a letter: and if Bill is all that she supposes
h m to be, then you will always ne sure of each other, and always
sure of Him. Your news pleases me well…

    … (I have a new ribbon, and a friend has offered to put it on this
machine for me. I have no doubt she will. ut when?

I forge t w hat I have written, nd cant read it: So this may be a
queer sort of letter. ut anyway, you have my love and best wishes

                        ay yours e a long and a happy union

                            I m your loving aunt Sally

Naturally, with such a wonderfully positive attitude, Sally had a constant
stream of visitors. Here is how the Reverend Desmond Gilliland, who had
served with her in China, remembers her when he called in the 1970's:

> When I knew her, in old age, there was an incandescence about
> her, which together with her legendary history of selfless devotion
> struck one with a sense of awe. The lively Cork accent and
> humour dispersed the halo to some extent, but not the quality.
>
> My own final impression was of her total possession of herself in
> old age, completely at ease, happy and thankful, marvelling at
> how privileged she was in her bedridden sojourn in St Luke's

Home - and always enquiring after the swans on the Bandon River! I always came away impregnated with her presence and humbled and proud of the association.

The Reverend Tom Kingston and his wife Gillian were also constant visitors during this period. They, too, recall a calm, happy woman, one whose mind was still sharp enough to notice when Tom accidentally misread a word in the Bible.

Sally died on 15th July, 1975, aged ninety. She was buried in St Finbarr's churchyard, which lies beside the Church of Ireland Cathedral of that name in Cork city.

The undertakers provided something for her funeral which I have never seen before or since - a silver-coloured hearse. It created one minor funny incident which would have appealed to Sally's sense of humour. As the cortège drove from the Wesley Chapel to the graveyard, two girls, standing on the roadside and obviously quite unused to silver hearses, tried to hitch a lift in it. The horror on their faces when they realised what they had done was quite graphic.

In her will, Sally left her few humble possessions to her immediate family but her money was given to the Methodist Missionary Society of London, to use 'for women's work'. The sum amounted to about a thousand pounds.

I have always understood that she took only half her pension, saying she had no need of more. Every penny saved, every thing she denied herself, was seen as a contribution made to her life's work and towards that of the Missionary Society.

This extract, found in her sister Fan's diary and dated 5th February, 1950, sums up the impact of that work:

> ... Ned met a missionary who knew Sally in China and he said her influence with the Chinese was wonderful. The people flock to their doors, he said, just to see her pass.

INDEX

*   Probably the same as Miss Li, see above.